By the same author:

   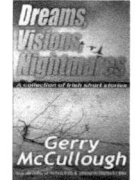

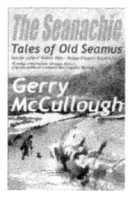   

Cover painting: *'Dunseverick'*, by **Ken Riddles**, Bangor, NI
Cover design: Raymond McCullough

The Seanachie 7

In the Spring ...
and other stories

Gerry McCullough

Published by

Precious Oil
PUBLICATIONS
www.preciousoil.com/publications

ISBN 13: 978-1-7384365-3-8

ISBN 10: 1-7384365-3-5

10a Listooder Road, Crossgar,

Downpatrick, Northern Ireland BT30 9JE

Contents

Introduction

The first story I ever had published was *A Tale of a Teacup*, in the all Ireland magazine, *Ireland's Own*. This was the first Old Seamus story, and it's included in my earlier collection, *The Seanachie: Tales of Old Seamus*. Because of this I have a very soft spot in my heart for it, and for all my Old Seamus stories. I've written 94 of them by now, and will go on writing them as long as my editor wants me to, and as long as the ideas keep coming.

I love the setting and the atmosphere. Whenever I start to create a Tale of Old Seamus, it's as if I've been transported not only to the Irish county of Donegal but to the days of long ago, when Seamus himself was younger and when life was simpler and happier. Donegal is a beautiful place, ideal for a holiday, wild and relaxing.

Above all, I love Old Seamus himself, and his happy-go-lucky attitude to life. Seamus gets by without a nine to five job, and enjoys himself day by day. He makes a living from poaching and by keeping hens and bees. He doesn't allow anyone to order him around or tell him what he should do. He has his own ideas about right and wrong, which mainly focus on helping people in trouble.

My first person narrator, Jamie, is a young man who loves to go up to Donegal, as he often explains, to get away from his busy city job, and to stay in the little white-washed cottage which he inherited from his grandparents, in the fictional Donegal village of Ardnakil.

As a child he often visited his grandparents there, and it was at that time that he first made friends with Seamus O'Hare, that disreputable old rogue, poacher and rascal, who taught Jamie everything he knows about the animals and flowers of the countryside. Seamus is an inveterate storyteller – which is what *Seanachie* means in Irish – and he loves to sit back, relax, and tell yet another story from his past. Jamie loves to listen – and I hope you will, too!

In this collection we have stories from Seamus' childhood, adolescence and from more recent times. Being kind-hearted Seamus often tries to help out his friends – not always with the expected consequences, though. His match-making attempts don't always work out as intended, either – for instance in the title story, '*In The Spring …* ' and again in, '*Curly Hair*'. Other times Seamus turns detective – to uncover a horse thief in, '*Seamus and the Horse Trader*'; and to retrieve a lost recipe in, '*The Christmas Pudding Recipe*'. He rescues one friend from serious trouble in, '*Flying Flynn*', and another from being defrauded in, '*Seamus and the Medicine Man.*'

I've enjoyed writing these stories. Hope you enjoy reading them!

Gerry McCullough

1 – The Silver Goblet

I was looking forward to my short break in Donegal, at the small white-washed cottage left to me by my grandparents, in the little village of Ardnakil. It had been a hard few months' slog since I'd last visited what was probably my favourite spot on earth. I whistled cheerfully to myself as I pulled my car into the village, then turned off into a side lane to arrive finally at my destination.

The lanes were no longer edged with a profusion of wild flowers, but a scattering of honeysuckle and white columbine still remained in the hedgerows, and clusters of blackberries and rose hips were to be seen, shining brightly where not long ago the wild roses had blossomed, while red haws gleamed from the hawthorn, making me realise that Autumn with its abundance was fast approaching. I heaved my suitcase out of the car, took it indoors, and sighed with content. I would light a turf fire later on, but just now all I wanted was to wander back down to the shops, pick up some food, and possibly run into my old friend Seamus O'Hare.

I met Seamus as I strolled around the village. He was wandering along happily with his disreputable old hat pushed to the back of his head, his curly white hair and beard surrounding his brown, sunburnt, wrinkled old face. I'd known Seamus since I used to come up to visit my grandparents when I was a child, and it was he who had taught me the names of birds and plants and had related a fund of stories besides.

'Seamus!' I exclaimed. 'Great to see you. How's about coming back with me and I'll give you a bite to eat when I've got the fire lit?'

'Sounds good, boy,' Seamus agreed, 'but I'll light the fire while you organise the food, see?'

'Division of labour,' I laughed. 'Many hands make light work. Okay. Let's do that.'

We turned back down the lane and were soon inside my cottage. Seamus got busy with turf, sticks and matches, while I filled the kettle and put it on the stove to make tea, and unwrapped, cut and buttered the soda bread I'd bought, still warm from the baker. In a short time we were sitting comfortably one on each side of the glowing fire, drinking our tea and munching our soda bread.

'So, Seamus, what have you been doing with yourself since I last saw you?' I asked him.

'Aw, Jamie, I couldn't begin to tell you everything. I had a visit from a young cousin of mine, a few weeks ago.'

'I didn't know you had any cousins, Seamus.'

'I don't have any living locally, Jamie, but this young lad was on a visit from Canada. He's gone on to see the rest of the country now. I knew his father Joe well, in fact he was one of my closest friends, but I haven't seen him since he moved out to Canada with his mother and father and his sister, when he was still very young, as I was myself. Aw, he was a great lad, was Joe. Always wanting to help people.'

'A bit like yourself, then, Seamus.'

'Maybe so, Jamie, but I hope I don't make such a mess of the helping as poor old Joe used to do. He got things so mixed up, for all his good intentions, that he often did more harm than good, I'm afraid. I could tell you many a story about him and the things he got up to.'

'Well, why don't you go ahead, Seamus, and tell me at least one, then.'

So Seamus settled himself back in the comfortable armchair, stretched out his legs, took another sip of tea, and began:

'Joe had a little sister called Kathleen whom he was very fond of. He didn't trust her an inch, though. According to Joe, she was always up to something, and he spent a lot of his time trying to save her from the consequences of her silly behaviour. I remember one particular time, the worst of the lot, when he came rushing round to see me one evening, and took something out of his big coat pocket which he insisted on showing me. It was a very impressive silver goblet, and looked as if it would be worth quite a lot of money.

'Heavens above, where did you get that, Joe?' I exclaimed.'I didn't get it,' Joe told me bitterly. 'My daft wee sister Kathleen got it! She must have stolen it, Seamus, for she could never have afforded to buy something like this herself.'

'But, Joe,' I said, pretty shocked at him, 'you surely don't believe that wee Kathleen's a thief?'

'I don't know what to believe, Seamus,' Joe said. 'You remember she used to nick sweeties from the village shop when she was just about able to walk?'

'Ah, but, Joe, a few sweeties when she wasn't much more than a baby is a very different thing from a silver cup like this.'

'I don't know,' replied Joe gloomily. 'Why had she hidden it in her schoolbag, then? Anyway, the point is, Seamus, what am I going to do with it? I need to get it back to its owner before they realise it's gone, if I possibly can.'

'And who is its owner, Joe?'

'That's one problem, Seamus. I'm not sure. But she was round visiting old Liam Flaherty just before I noticed it in her bag, so I'm guessing it's his.'

Liam Flaherty was a wealthy man, quite elderly and not in the best of health. He lived in a big house on the edge of the village, and his front room was full of large glass cases packed with the valuable silver objects which he'd been collecting for years. Kathleen, out of the goodness of her heart, had been visiting him regularly, just to chat and keep him company, for he'd been a friend of her granny and granda before they died, and she knew him well. He was an obstinate, bad tempered old man, with few friends still living, so Kathleen's visits were very welcome to him.

'Joe, you aren't planning to accuse her, are you?' I asked him.

'Well, no, but I thought I'd have a talk with her after I've put it back. I can't just let her get away with it, can I? She'd go on doing the same sort of thing again, unless I give her a bit of a talking to. I'll need to be tactful, though, won't I?'

I laughed inwardly, for if there's one thing Joe is sadly lacking in, it's tact. 'So, you aren't going to tell Liam Flaherty she took it, I hope?' I said anxiously.

'No, I don't want to give her away,' Joe admitted. 'But, Seamus, I don't know how I'm going to do this. Will you help me?'

'Indeed I will, Joe,' I said. 'But what to you mean to do?'

'I thought you might have some ideas, Seamus?'

'Well, I suppose – ' I thought, then I said, 'Suppose you and me call round with him after school tomorrow, Joe, just to say hullo, sort of, and I'll keep him talking while you make some excuse and sneak into his front room where he has all the silver in the big glass cases, and put it in whichever one has a space. And let's just pray he hasn't noticed yet that it's gone.'

Joe's face brightened up. 'That sounds like a great idea, Seamus!' he said. 'Right, you're on. Tomorrow after school.'

After Joe had gone, I sat by the fire thinking. I found it hard to believe Kathleen would have done such a thing. I'd known her since she was born, and apart from the sweeties business, she'd always been honest. She was a couple of years younger than Joe and me, which made her about twelve – quite old enough to know better.

As I was thinking, I heard a soft knock on the door, and a voice calling out, 'Are you there, Seamus? Can I come in? It's Kathleen.'

'Come away in, Kathleen!' I called back to her. 'The door's on the latch,' and a moment later her fresh young face surrounded with bushy brown hair was peeping round the door at me. She came in with a rush, sat down beside me on the hearth, and burst out, 'Oh, Seamus, I don't know what to do! It's Joe! He's stolen something! At least, I think it must have been him, because there was nobody else in the house at the time!'

'Now, now, Kathleen, calm yourself,' I said. 'Sure, you know rightly that Joe would be the last person to steal something.'

'But there was nobody else there,' Kathleen wailed. 'I brought my bag home this afternoon, and no one else was in. And when I looked at it a while ago, the silver goblet had disappeared. There was no one but Joe could have taken it!'

'The silver goblet?' I asked her sharply. 'What were you doing with a silver goblet, Kathleen?'

Kathleen looked worried, then her face cleared. 'It's supposed to be a secret, Seamus, so you must promise not to tell,' she said solemnly.

'All right, Kathleen, I promise.'

'Well, Liam Flaherty gave it to me, when I was round there earlier. He wants to donate it to the church, but he doesn't want anyone to know it came from him. He quoted me some stuff about not letting your right hand know what your left is doing, but to tell you the truth' – she giggled, and looked mischievous – 'he had a big quarrel with Father Donnelly, the last time he called round, and I think it's really that he doesn't want Father Donnelly to think he's trying to make it up with him – you know how obstinate Liam is! So I'm supposed to take it round, but not let on where it came from. As if everyone won't know at once! Who else round here has so much silver he can afford to give it away?'

We both laughed, but then Kathleen's face suddenly fell again. 'Oh, Seamus, it's no laughing matter! What on earth am I going to do?'

'Don't worry, Kathleen,' I said, trying to comfort her. 'You just do nothing until you hear from me, girl. I'll have a word with Joe and see if I can find out if he really took the goblet, and if he has it I'll get it back for you.'

'But, Seamus, you won't go and accuse him of stealing it, will you? I don't want him to know I think he took it.'

'I'll be as tactful as I can,' I promised her, thinking that this business seemed to be needing a huge amount of tact, one way or the other. 'Now, you run away home, and not a word to Joe, mind you. I'll talk to him tomorrow.'

When Kathleen had gone, looking a bit more cheerful, I sat on by the fire for some time, thinking out what would be the best thing to do. When I'd come to a conclusion I made my way to bed.

Next afternoon, Joe called round for me as we'd arranged. It had been such a beautiful day that I hadn't been able to resist the urge to go fishing instead of being stuck in school, and besides, I needed something like a nice fresh fish for my tea, so although Joe had been to school as always, I hadn't, and we hadn't seen each other yet.

'Come away in, Joe, and let's talk,' I said to him, drawing him into the cottage. 'Sit down there by the fire, while I tell you something. First of all, have you got the silver goblet with you?'

'Of course I have, Seamus,' said Joe, looking surprised. 'Wasn't it the whole idea that I'd bring it with me to put back?'

'And you haven't said anything to Kathleen yet?'

'Seamus, you know that was what we agreed!'

'All right, Joe. That's fine. Now, I've a secret to tell you, and you mustn't repeat it.'

And without more ado I told him what Kathleen had told me. Joe was thunderstruck.

His first reaction was relief. 'Thank goodness she didn't steal it after all, Seamus,' he exclaimed. Then his face clouded over with dismay. 'But, Seamus!' he wailed, 'what'll I say to her? I don't want her to know that I thought she was a thief!'

'Then don't tell her that!' I said briskly. 'Tell her you put it away for safety, and forgot to mention it to her.' For that was the only idea I'd been able to come up with.

'But, Seamus, she'll think me a right eedjit, forgetting to tell her about something so important.'

'I suppose she will, Joe,' I said calmly. 'But it's your own fault. Fancy thinking a good wee girl like Kathleen was a thief! Maybe you'll think twice the next time before you jump to such conclusions.'

And, do you know, I do believe that he did.

2 – The Christmas Pudding Recipe

I rubbed my hands together for warmth and shivered a little. It was the Christmas season, so the weather was chilly. It seemed particularly cold in my little whitewashed cottage in the small village of Ardnakil in Donegal, but once I got the turf fire roaring, I knew, it would heat up amazingly. The flames licked round the turf and caught, and I stood up, satisfied.

'There you are, Seamus,' I said. 'That'll soon warm us up.'

I had been walking through the fields with my old friend Seamus O'Hare, until a sudden flurry of snowflakes had sent us hurrying to my cottage.

I'd known Seamus since I was a child, when I used to come to visit my grandparents in this same cottage which they had now left to me. Though he was a bit of a rogue, and made his living by poaching, Seamus had a heart of gold. He was also a *Seanachie*, that is a storyteller in Irish, and I was always happy to hear another of his tales.

We settled ourselves by the fire with cups of tea, and Seamus produced from one of his capacious pockets a bag of shortbread biscuits. I took one, bit into it and found that it was unusually delicious.

'My friend Sarah Gallagher gave me these,' he told me. 'Sarah's a great cook, and she's always very generous to me, for she thinks I did her a really good turn, many years ago.'

'And did you, Seamus?'

'Well, I suppose I did,' Seamus admitted. 'Although it wasn't her so much as my friend the Honourable Marjorie I was trying to help. You've heard me mention the Hon. Marjorie, haven't you?'

'Indeed I have,' I said. 'When you were helping another friend of yours, Annie, who didn't want to leave her cottage and her apple tree. The Hon. Marjorie ended up thinking you'd helped her instead.'

'Ah, indeed. She's given me the run of her river ever since. Those were the days!' he sighed nostalgically.

'So, are you going to tell me this story about Sarah Gallagher, then, Seamus?' I settled back in my chair to listen, helping myself to another shortbread biscuit, and Seamus began:

Sarah, as I told you, was a great cook, and she worked for the Hon. Marjorie. This was in the days when people had cooks – at least, people like the Hon. Marjorie. Marjorie could always be sure that when she invited guests round, they would have a very nice meal, especially at Christmas time, when Sarah was at her best.

She had a special recipe, handed down her family for generations, for Christmas Pudding, and it was certainly the best I've ever tasted. But one day, not long before Christmas, I called in on the Hon Marjorie and found her very upset. She wasn't in tears, for she wasn't the sort of person who broke down and cried, but that was the most you could say.

'Why, Marjorie, what on earth's the matter?' I asked her, feeling really concerned, and expecting to hear of a death in the family or at least serious illness. But, no.

'It's Sarah, my cook!' the Hon Marjorie moaned. 'She's leaving me. And twenty people coming for Christmas dinner!'

"She was a good cook, as cooks go. And as cooks go, she went," I quoted flippantly. Marjorie turned on me.

'It's not funny, Seamus O'Hare. Can't you do something about it instead of making silly jokes?'

I pulled myself together and looked serious. 'Well, who knows? Maybe if I knew why she was going I could talk her out of it.'

The Hon. Marjorie brightened up immediately. 'Seamus, that would be wonderful. I tell you what, come through to the kitchen and I'll let her explain the whole thing herself.'

So I followed her into the kitchen, where, to my annoyance, she announced, 'Here's Seamus come to see you, Sarah!' and left me to it.

Sarah was sitting dolefully at her huge kitchen table, her dog Dandy, a sweet natured dachshund, on her knee. Like most good cooks, she was a plump, red cheeked woman, who usually looked comfortable, good natured and cheerful. But now, she looked up as I came in and just about managed to smile at me. I went over and stroked Dandy.

'Now, what's all this about, Sarah?' I asked her.

'It's my Christmas Pudding recipe, Seamus. Some villain's stolen it. My mammy handed it down to me on her deathbed, and made me swear an oath that I'd never show it or tell it to anyone except one person in the next generation of the family. I was to choose the most suitable one, and be sure they took it seriously, and swore the same oath I did. Mammy said the recipe went back at least to her great-great-granny, if not further. And now it's gone!'

I tut tutted and dear, deared for a bit, then I asked her, 'Where did you see it last, Sarah?'

'Where I always kept it,' Sarah told me, 'Tucked into my big recipe book. I never needed to take it out to look at, because I know it by heart, so it never moves from its proper place. But now it's gone. Look. I'll show you the book.'

She got up, setting Dandy on the floor, went to fetch an enormous book, *Mrs Beaton's Book of Household Management*, from the shelf against the far wall, and opened it to show me. There were a number of cuttings inserted into the various pages of the book, and as Sarah set it on the table, a couple of them drifted out and fell. Sarah picked them up automatically, just in time to stop Dandy pouncing on them, and tucked them back in the book.

'I know exactly which page it should be at,' Sarah said. 'I noticed at once it wasn't there, when I checked the recipe for mince pies yesterday, because that's where I've always kept it. Some villain's stolen it,' she repeated, 'and I'm not staying here in Ardnakil any longer, where thieves break in and take what they like. I'm going back to my own place, Millerstown, where people are honest and you can trust them not to take your dearest possessions.'

'Have you ever taken the book out of this kitchen, Sarah?' I asked her, for the idea that a thief should have broken into the house and stolen nothing but a Christmas Pudding recipe seemed to me pretty unlikely.

'Oh, yes, I have, and if no one got into this house to steal it, that's when it must have been done,' Sarah burst out. 'And that makes it even worse! I took it with me to a talk I gave to the Ardnakil Women's Meeting recently. I put it down on the table for a few minutes while they were giving me a cup of tea and introducing me to two new members. But I thought those women were all my friends.

I was so pleased to be asked to speak to them. And if one of them stole my recipe, I never want to have anything more to do with them or anyone else in this dreadful place. I'm leaving!'

There didn't seem to be anything more I could say to change her mind. It certainly seemed likely that one of the women at that meeting had taken the recipe, but even if I could find out which one had done it, Sarah would still feel the same sense of betrayal of friendship. I patted her hand and said I would go away and have a think about it, and then I went back to the Hon Marjorie and said much the same to her.

'I don't see what I can do, Marjorie,' I admitted to her, 'but I'll do my best to come up with something.'

Then I went away and thought.

To make matters worse, I ran into Martha Gilmore, that year's president of the Women's Meeting, as I was making my way home, and the first thing she said to me was to ask if it was true that Sarah's recipe had gone missing after her talk to them. 'How dreadful if my women are suspected of stealing it!' she exclaimed. 'In my year of being president. I'll never get over it.'

'Well, Martha, it wouldn't be your fault,' I said reasonably. But she couldn't see it.

'It feels as if it was,' she said miserably. I'd known Martha for years and knew her as a bright, busy, little woman who never let anything get her down, but here was a third person unhappy and upset on account of this missing recipe.

'Can't you do something about it, Seamus?' she asked me. It seemed that I'd got myself a reputation, somehow or other, for working miracles. I wished all these people weren't expecting so much from me, especially as my mind seemed empty of ideas.

It was as I was going to bed that night, whistling to myself, that the glimmering of an idea came into my head. *'All things bright and beautiful, All creatures great and small, All things wise and wonderful, The Lord God made them all,'* I whistled, and then suddenly the idea came to me. I decided to go round to see Sarah the next day, and find out if there was anything in it.

Just after lunch, leaving time for Sarah to clear away and wash up, and eat her own lunch, I went round, and told the Hon Marjorie that, while she shouldn't hold her breath, I might have an idea. Then I went to the kitchen, and there was Sarah, sitting with Dandy on her knee. I had brought a rubber chewing toy for Dandy, and I threw it to him as I came in.

'Here, boy!'

He was down from Sarah's knee in a minute, pouncing on the chew. I left him to get on with it, while I sat down to talk to Sarah, asking her a few unimportant questions. 'If you knew for sure, Sarah, that no one in Ardnakil took your recipe, would that make you happy about staying?' I said eventually. I was watching Dandy out of the corner of my eye.

'I don't see how that could be,' was all Sarah said. I saw that Dandy had taken the chew over to his basket and was busily inserting it under his blanket.

'You'd be surprised,' I said. Then I got up and went over to Dandy. 'Does he always hide his treasures under this blanket?' I asked Sarah.

'Why – mostly,' she answered. A spark of realisation came into her eye. 'You don't think –?' Her voice tailed off, and she watched me eagerly as I lifted Dandy gently to one side and began to explore his basket, lifting up the spread blanket to reveal the crumpled up newspaper which Sarah had used to provide a base.

There, standing out clearly to both our eyes, was a blank sheet of paper, quite different from the newspaper bundles. I took it up and looked at the other side. It was the missing recipe.

'Your property, ma'am,' I said gravely, handing it to Sarah.

The look on her face was reward enough for the small amount of trouble I'd taken. She seized it and read it again and again, then she grabbed me and started hugging me and kissing me.

'Oh, Seamus, what can I do to thank you?'

'That's easy – let me tell the Hon. Marjorie that you've changed your mind about leaving, that you're going to stay on right here as her cook.'

'Oh, of course I am! How could I ever have thought of leaving this lovely place! And how could I have been so stupid! I should have thought of Dandy hiding it in his basket right at the start. He always tries to get hold of anything I drop. He must have taken it without me noticing. It must have fallen out when I was leafing through my book, for ideas for my talk to the Ardnakil Women's Meeting.'

I knew that, because I'd seen Dandy trying to seize on a couple of dropped recipes the previous day, but I hadn't known where he would hide one. That's why I'd brought him the chew.

I left Sarah hugging Dandy in turn and telling him he was a bad, naughty boy, but in the kind of loving tone that wasn't going to make him behave any differently in future, and went to tell the Hon. Marjorie that her dinner party was safe.

I knew that I wouldn't get any hugs or kisses from Marjorie, but she was pretty pleased all the same, and the next day a huge salmon from her river arrived on my doorstep – and she's been extra generous to me ever since. Martha Gilmore got back her beaming smile, too, so I'd made three women happy in one day.

And that's why you're sitting there wolfing up Sarah's shortbread, boy. Go on – have another piece. There'll be plenty more arriving before long!'

3 – In the Spring ...

Although it was not quite spring, Spring was in the air. The sky was a pale blue, a fresh breeze raised my spirits, and the green meadows were dotted with purple, gold and white crocuses, as I strolled near my small whitewashed cottage in the little Donegal village of Ardnakil. I whistled My Lagan Love, and remembered the words of Tennyson's poem,

'In the Spring a young man's fancy

Lightly turns to thoughts of love.'

I was a young man, and for too long I'd been fancy free. It would be nice to meet the right girl.

I turned aside to call on my old friend Seamus O'Hare at his tumbledown home. I'd known Seamus since, as a child, I visited my grandparents in the cottage they had since left me. Seamus was a rogue, a poacher, but with a heart of gold, and he was also a *Seanachie*, or story teller. I always enjoyed the continual flow of stories he told me.

'Are you home, Seamus?' I called as I made my way up the path through the wilderness that was his garden and looked in at the open top of his half door.

'Indeed and I am, boy,' Seamus called back. 'Come away on in!'

I was glad to see a bright turf fire on his hearth, for pleasant though the day was, there was a nip in the air.

Seamus offered me a cup of tea straightaway, and while he was making it I glanced around happily at the familiar room. A snapshot I had never noticed before caught my eye, a lovely girl with a pale Irish face, long black hair and blue grey eyes with a black rim round the iris. I thought I'd never seen a more beautiful girl, and smiled as I recalled my recent thoughts.

'Who's the girl in the photo, Seamus?' I asked him. 'And why haven't I seen it before?'

'Well, you haven't seen it before because it came in the post yesterday,' Seamus explained with a mischievous twinkle. His brown weather beaten old face was wreathed in smiles. 'As for who she is, it's the daughter of one of my American friends. I have a lot of friends in America. They sometimes send me photos, and I put them in my album, but I hadn't got round to putting this one away yet.'

'They come to visit you sometimes, don't they?' I said, remembering some of his stories. 'Well, if this girl tells you she's coming, let me know and I'll make a point of being here, so I can meet her.'

Seamus laughed. 'I'll do that, Jamie. But you might find her a disappointment in the flesh.'

'I don't think so, Seamus.'

'You remind me of my young friend Malachi O'Peake. Mal saw a photo I had, and was crazy to meet the girl.'

'So, are you going to tell me Mal's story, Seamus?' I settled back at the fireside with my cup of tea and prepared to listen as Seamus began his story:

'Mal was a nice young fella. He had a small farm his da had left him, not far from here, and it was a wonder to everyone that he hadn't married long since, for he could well afford it.But Mal was fussy when it came to choosing a wife, and not one of the local girls suited him.

Indeed, I was beginning to wonder if he'd ever find the right one, until one day, like yourself, he called in with me and saw a snapshot I'd chanced to be looking at. I'd been sent it a few months before, but sure it was probably still what the girl looked like. Her name was Maureen Murphy, and she had red curly hair and a sweet cheeky look to her. Mal fell for her like a ton of bricks, and nothing would do for him but to meet her.

'You could invite her to come over for a visit, Seamus,' he urged me. 'Go on, why not?'

It seemed a harmless thing to do, and I told Mal I'd write that night.

Maureen seemed delighted by the invitation, and wrote that she'd been planning to come to Ireland very soon, and would love to call and see me, so that was settled. I told Mal, and he was more than pleased. I couldn't help thinking he might be disappointed when he actually met her. And she might not be particularly keen on him.

Mal decided that he needed to let Maureen see him at his best, so he went into Millerstown on the bus and bought himself some new clothes. But when he looked at himself in the shop mirror, he still wasn't satisfied. He asked me what more he could do.

I looked at him and smiled. 'Well, since you're asking me, boy, if I were you I'd get myself a decent haircut. Something with a bit of shape to it.' For Mal had been getting the woman who cleaned for him to give him a trim from time to time, using a pudding bowl paced upside down over his head to help her judge where to cut. The result, known locally as a *'pudding bowl haircut'* didn't do a lot for him.

Mal brightened up. 'I'll do that, Seamus,' he said.

So in his next free time Mal went along to *Barney's Cuts*, as the local hairdresser's was called. Barney had taken over recently from Sylvia, a friend of mine. I hadn't met him, but he seemed a cross grained fella, from what I'd heard about him.

To Mal's surprise, for he'd never crossed the threshold before, he found that Barney cut hair for both men and women. In fact he cut, curled and coloured, and he had a young girl to help him, for the local people kept him busy enough.

Barney, who was with a customer, greeted Mal when he came in, but said, 'Maybe you'll wait over there for a few minutes, Malachi.' Barney made it his business to know as many people in Ardnakil as he could. They liked to be greeted by name, he always said, if and when they decided to come in. 'Sally'll be finished shortly, and she'll help you.'

Mal was a bit thunderstruck to learn that his hair would be cut by a girl, but he decided that he would go along with it. After all, maybe it was usual. What did he know about hairdressers? And presently Sally's customer left, and Sally came over and put a plastic wrap round his shoulders and led him to one of the chairs.

'What can I do for you, sir?' she asked in a quavering voice. Mal looked at her sharply, and noticed that her eyes were red as if she'd been crying. His soft heart was immediately touched.

'Is there something wrong, lass?' he asked gruffly.

'Hush!' Sally whispered. 'Don't let my uncle Barney hear you. Was it a haircut you were wanting, sir?'

'Yes, a haircut, Sally. But don't be calling me sir – my name's Malachi O'Peake, or Mal.'

'Okay, then, Mal it is.' Sally smiled at him in the mirror, and Mal realised for the first time what a pretty girl she was. She had short fair hair curled round her face, her eyes were very blue in spite of their red rims, and there was a sweet innocence about her.

Sally took her time cutting his hair, going about it very carefully, and Mal was just beginning to think with pleasure that he seemed to look quite handsome for once, when Barney came over to see how she was getting on, and said in an unnecessarily loud and unpleasant voice, right in her ear, 'What's keeping you, girl? There's another customer waiting.'

Sally, who had been concentrating on the final few cuts, hadn't noticed his approach. At the sound of his voice in her ear she jumped, the scissors slipped, and next moment the blood was spouting from Mal's ear, where she had nicked him.

Now, it was far from being a serious cut. It looked worse than it was, because ears bleed so freely. Sally grabbed a handful of tissues from the nearby box and began to mop Mal up, apologising feverishly as she did, and Mal tried to turn the incident off with a laugh and a joke, saying, 'Missed my throat that time, Sally! You'll have to try again!' but Barney had no idea of letting it pass so lightly.

'I can't apologise enough, sir,' he said to Mal. 'That's the second time this clumsy girl has hurt a customer. Well, there's no place for clumsy hairdressers at *Barney's Cuts*. Out she goes. I've warned her once, and once was enough. You'll go straight back to your mother this afternoon, you stupid girl, and don't expect any more help from me!'

Mal stood up and put his arm round Sally, who by now was weeping bitterly. 'That's enough of that, Barney,' he said sternly. 'I'm not hurt. If it was anyone's fault it was yours, coming up and shouting at Sally, making her jump. Don't cry, Sally. You're well out of this place, even if Barney is your uncle. C'mon, I'll pay for the great haircut and then we'll go and get you a cup of tea in the cafe.'

Over the cup of tea, Sally explained that her mother was a widow with other younger children to support, so that it had been a real blessing when Uncle Barney had offered to give Sally a job in his salon. 'It meant that I was self supporting, and even able to send some money home. Not that it was much, for I wasn't earning much while I was still being trained. I'd never cut hair in my life before I got this job.'

'Well, Sally, it sounds to me as if your uncle Barney has been taking advantage of you. You're well out of it.'

'But what will I do now?' Sally asked woefully. And as she raised her tear-filled blue eyes trustingly to his face, Mal had an inspiration.

'You'll come and be my housekeeper, Sally,' he said firmly. 'I've been needing one for some times, and I can give you a better wage than your skinflint old uncle.'

'Oh, Mal, that would be lovely!' breathed Sally rapturously. Looking at her, Mal was sure it would be, too. And, all right, it was a bit soon yet, but maybe before too long Sally would agree to be Mrs Malachi O'Peake. Somehow, he thought she would. (And he was right.)

Later that evening, a very guilty looking Mal called round to explain why he wouldn't be coming to meet Maureen after all. 'And I can't stay, Seamus. I have to get back to Sally. I left her unpacking. But I just wanted to tell you that I'm sorry for putting you to the trouble of inviting Maureen for nothing.'

Well, I was sorry, too. I was pleased for Mal. Sally sounded nice. But I hoped Maureen hadn't been expecting anything. Not that I'd mentioned Mal to her, but she probably thought there was something behind my sudden invitation. So I was nervous enough when she turned up as arranged a few days later.

She came flying in when I opened the door for her, as full of energy as her photo had led me to expect.

'Oh, Seamus, it's great to see you again!' she cried out. 'It's years since you used to set me on your knee and tell me stories.'

It was, and looking at the weight she'd put on, I reflected that I wouldn't like to have her on my knee now, for I'd be squashed flat. Then looking at her again, I realised the reason for her weight. She was clearly pregnant.

I didn't know what to say. I'm not easily shocked, but I just hadn't known. I was glad Mal had found Sally.

'Hadn't you better sit down, Maureen, lass?' I said. 'When are you due?'

'Another four months, Seamus.'

I cast around for something to say. 'Well,' I said at last, 'A baby is always a blessing from the Lord, whatever the circumstances.'

Maureen realised what I'd been thinking. 'Didn't you know I was married, Seamus?' She laughed. 'The baby must have been quite a shock to you, then. This trip to Ireland is a sort of late honeymoon for my husband Jack and me. Jack'll be along shortly, he's been leaving our things at *The Golden Pheasant*.'

I had recovered myself enough by now to smile at her and ask, 'So is it a boy or a girl, Maureen? If it's a boy, you'll have to promise me to call him Seamus.'

'We don't know yet, Seamus. We wanted a surprise. We'll love whatever the Lord sends. But Jack's sure it's a boy, because he has a kick like a professional footballer!' She sprang up and came over. 'Seamus, I must give you a hug!'

And as she put her arms round me, standing close, wee Seamus kicked me firmly in the stomach.

4 – Curly Hair

I sat with my friend Seamus O'Hare in *The Golden Pheasant* bar, in the main street of the little Donegal village of Ardnakil, looking through the open door at sunshine splashing across the road and foot-path, and the river sparkling along, as the sun slipping slyly through the doorway spread itself out comfortably over the old flagstones of the floor.

I had come up for a weekend break to the whitewashed cottage left to me by my grandparents. I'd visited them there as a child, and got to know Seamus. He had told me all about the countryside, the animals, the flowers, plants and trees, the bird song. Seamus knew all these things. He was a poacher, but he had a heart of gold and would always help anyone who needed it. He had a host of stories besides, was a real Seanachie, and would keep me entertained regularly. I always enjoyed spending time with him.

'The river looks really beautiful, Seamus,' I said idly. 'Does any-one ever take a boat out on it, or is it left to itself? Have you been out on it, for instance?'

'Oh, I've been out on it, boy,' Seamus told me. 'In fact, I could tell you a story or two about my times on the river, if you like.'

'Oh, I'd like to hear any story you have to tell, Seamus,' I said heartily. 'Go ahead, why don't you?'

'Well, it's partly to do with my friend, Gavin Randal,' Seamus began:

'Gavin was a great guy, and I'd known him for years. He'd been away working in a bank in Dublin for a while, and he'd recently come back to a senior job in the branch in Millerstown. Only a short time before that, Mary McBride, whom I'd known when she was at school with me and Gavin, had come back to Ardnakil when her husband died, and the story is about her, too.

And it's about Peter O'Hanlon as well, another old school mate, a shy little boy when I knew him. His parents, who'd lived to a right old age, had died not long ago, and Peter had come back to run the farm they left him.

Peter and Gavin were both keen on Mary, as far as I could see. They were all much the same age, around fifty, as I was myself at that time. Mary was still a pretty woman, sweet and good natured, the sort of wife anyone might like to have. I wasn't surprised at either Gavin or Peter, but to me, there was very little to choose between them. Both good fellows, not bad looking. The only advantage one had over the other was that Peter had a mop of dark curly hair which at least doubled his attractiveness.

One evening I was sitting in my garden enjoying the last of the evening sunshine when Gavin called round.

'I don't know what to do about Mary, Seamus,' he burst out suddenly after sitting in gloomy silence for a while. 'I don't seem to be getting anywhere with her. I can't get her on her own. Peter O'Hanlon is always there, hanging round, and how can I propose to her if he's always there? I can't even invite her to come for a walk, without Peter assuming he's included too. And Mary has such a kind heart she won't tell him to go away.'

'Well, Gavin, maybe he's thinking just the same about you,' I said. 'If Mary was ready to listen to you, don't you think she'd make an opportunity, or say something to Peter, kind heart or not? Maybe she just doesn't know which of you to have – if either.'

'I know,' Gavin said, sounding even more gloomy. 'I've heard her say she loves curly hair, thinks it's very attractive – and Peter certainly has curly hair, far too much of it in my opinion.'

'Do I hear a note of jealousy, Gavin?' I asked him with a mischievous chuckle.

'You do, Seamus, you do,' Gavin groaned. 'How am I going to compete with that?' He sat silently for a few minutes, then brightened up. 'I'm sure I could talk her into taking me if I could just get a bit of time alone with her, Seamus,' he said. 'I want to ask you a favour. Could you arrange with Peter to go out fishing or something like that someday soon? After all, you were good friends with him at school, and you haven't seen much of him since he got back. What do you say?'

Chapter 4 – Curly Hair

Well, I was willing to help Gavin, although I wasn't as sure as he seemed to be that in a few hours alone with Mary McBride he'd win her heart. However, he deserved the chance. And I was happy enough to invite Peter to spend an afternoon fishing with me.

So when I next bumped into Peter, I invited him to join me for a day's fishing, taking out the rowing boat which my friend Dougie Flanaghan was always happy to lend me.

'That would be great, Seamus!' Peter said enthusiastically. 'I haven't been fishing, or out in a boat for that matter, for ages.'

We arranged to meet up on the riverbank a mile or so upriver from the village, and I was delighted to see that the weather favoured us on the day. But before that, Mary McBride called round to see me, and like Gavin, sat with me in the garden enjoying the evening sunshine.

'Och, it's nice to be back home again, Seamus,' she sighed after a bit of chit chat. 'But I'm having problems.'

'Oh?' I asked in an encouraging voice. 'Would you like to tell me about them?'

'Well, I suppose it's only one problem, really,' Mary said. Then it all came bubbling out. How both Gavin and Peter seemed very fond of her, and how she had always liked them, and now she didn't know what to do. 'Advise me, Seamus! I'm so mixed up. Gavin's so kind hearted. I'd hate to hurt his feelings. But you'd have to admit he isn't a patch on Peter, with all that dark curly hair –'

'Mary, looks aren't everything,' I interrupted her. 'It's up to yourself. No one else can tell you which of them you like best.'

'Well, you're right, there, Seamus,' she admitted. 'I'll go away and think some more about it. And thanks for listening, like a true friend, and giving me such good advice.'

The next day I met Peter, as arranged, and we loaded the boat with a picnic lunch which Peter had produced in a large well packed hamper, the fishing rods, and finally ourselves, and rowed out into the middle of the river.

We fished for some time and caught several trout between us.

'Enough for both our teas,' I said. 'If you like to come round later to my cottage we can fry them up with a few spuds from my garden.'

'Great idea, Seamus,' Peter agreed enthusiastically. 'But meanwhile, it's getting on for the middle of the afternoon – we should have had lunch ages ago.'

The fresh air had made us both hungry. 'You're right there, Peter,' I said. 'I'll row over to the bank and find somewhere to moor the boat. Then we can get started on this basket of yours. It looks as if it would feed an army!'

There was an overhanging tree on the nearest bank, its boughs drooping into the water. I made for that and pulled in under it. Just as I was attaching the mooring rope to the thickest branch, looping it round it, and about to fasten it, I caught sight of something out of the corner of my eye, and decided hastily that this wasn't the best place for us. It was Gavin sitting on a rug with Mary, at the far side of the tree. They didn't seem to have noticed us yet.

I wondered savagely why Gavin had been so stupid as to bring Mary here, knowing Peter and I would be fishing nearby, but I learned later that it had been her suggestion to walk by the river, and she had been quite obstinate about it. In the end, Gavin had decided that the best he could do was to bring a rug and persuade her to sit down after walking for a while, in a secluded spot where he hoped not to see us. But that wasn't how it worked out.

I thought it would be better if Peter didn't see them, or vice versa, so I said, beginning to unloop the rope hastily, 'I think we could find a better place than this, Peter. Let's row on a bit.'

'Och, Seamus, this is fine,' protested Peter. 'I'm starving! Let's get this picnic basket ashore.' And he stood up, starting to lift the basket.

Now, whether it was my fault or Peter's, or just that the boat wasn't properly attached to the branch by now, I don't know, but there was a jerk as the boat drifted sideways, Peter stumbled, the basket fell at his feet, and a moment later he was tripping over the boat's edge. I grabbed out at him, but I wasn't in time.

He went over into the water with an almighty splash. I wasn't much worried about him. I knew he could swim fine. But to my dismay, the sound of the splash had brought both Mary and Gavin round the tree, wanting to know what had happened, and if everything was all right.

And something else had happened. Somehow or other, one of the low hanging branches had caught in Peter's hair. And as he came safely back to the surface, I saw that his head was almost completely bald, except for a few wisps of wet grey hair. His dark curls were hanging from the tree. At the same moment, I heard Gavin exclaim, 'It's a wig! He was wearing a wig all the time, Mary!' And he burst into loud laughter.

My heart sank. Although I'd been trying to help Gavin, during the afternoon I'd spent with him, I'd realised how much more I actually liked Peter. He was quiet and shy, and he didn't push himself forward, but he was a great fishing companion, and we'd shared some jokes and happy memories. I hated to see him made a fool of. He didn't deserve that, even if he had been daft enough to wear a wig, probably to attract Mary, I thought. It seemed certain that Gavin would easily win Mary now, since the curly hair she'd loved in Peter was all make believe.

But you never can tell with a woman.

Mary was rushing forward, full of concern. 'Peter! Are you all right, Peter?' She helped him ashore, and tried to brush the water weeds off him. Then she turned on Gavin like a raging fury.

'There's nothing to laugh at! Peter might have been drowned. You're a heartless pig, and I wish you'd take yourself off back to Millerstown, where you can enjoy yourself laughing at all the people who want loans, before you turn them down. I'm sure you love doing that!'

'Mary, you've got me all wrong!' Gavin protested, and indeed I think for a bank manager he was a very decent fella. But it was too late for him to convince Mary of that. She was full of sympathy for Peter, curly hair or no curly hair.

'Come on, Peter, we'll have to get you home and into some dry clothes,' she insisted, and before either Gavin or I could say any more, she had taken him off to her own cottage, which was nearest, promising him a hot bath, warm towels, a fire and hot soup, and whatever else she could think off. 'I'll dry your clothes for you while you're recovering,' was the last we heard as they disappeared off along the path, leaving Peter's wig still hanging from the tree.

Gavin and I sat down gloomily to eat up the contents of the picnic basket, and later we went to my cottage and fried up the fish Peter and I had meant to share. 'Cheer up, boy,' I said to him. 'Women are funny creatures. But there are plenty more fish in the sea, to use an appropriate metaphor.'

And by the time he went home, I think he was feeling a bit better. 'I never thought she had a temper like that, Seamus,' was the last thing he said. 'Maybe I'm just as well without her!'

As for Peter and Mary, they never looked back. At their wedding shortly after, Mary told me she'd loved Peter for as long as she'd known him. But he'd been too shy to speak, so she'd married someone else.

'Better late than never, Seamus,' she laughed.

'And what about the curly hair, Mary?'

'Sure, he only wore the wig to impress me, Seamus. I think it was very sweet of him. And you were quite right – it's not curly hair. It's the person beneath it that matters.'

5 – The Charity Collector

It was a beautiful summer's day when I drove my little sports car through the green, grassy hills of Donegal, and came down into the village of Ardnakil, lying snugly in the sunshine beside the river and the trees. I had inherited a small whitewashed cottage there from my grandparents, and since I'd been coming to Ardnakil to visit them for many years before that, the place always felt like a second home to me.

I looked forward to meeting up with my old friend Seamus O'Hare, who had taught me everything I knew about the birds, plants and animals of the surrounding fields and woods, and had regularly entertained me with his fund of stories about himself or his friends. Seamus was a real *Seanachie*.

After lunch I wandered out to stroll through the leafy lanes, with their blossoming hedges and the wild flowers bright along their verges, to enjoy the country air, expecting to bump into Seamus somewhere. There was no sign of him, and after calling at his favourite watering hole, *The Golden Pheasant*, in vain, I decided that he might be at home in his tumbledown old cottage, although it wasn't like Seamus to be indoors on a day like this. However, he might be sitting in his garden, or tending his plants or animals.

I made for the cottage, and seeing no sign of him in the overgrown garden where the bees buzzed merrily from flower to flower, collecting honey for Seamus's hives, I knocked on his green half door and called in, 'Are you there, Seamus?'

'Is it yourself, Jamie, boy?' came Seamus's response. 'Come away on in!'

I pushed open the door and saw, to my surprise, that Seamus was in his tiny bedroom, no more than a closet off the main kitchen and living room. I'd never known him to be in bed in the middle of the day.

'Seamus, are you ill?' I asked in concern.

'Nearly better now, boy,' he assured me. 'A touch of bronchitis, that's all. But Nurse Annie McCracken has been looking after me, and my friends have been bringing me food and medicine, and making meals for me. Another day or two and nurse tells me I'll be out of bed and fit.'

'Well, I'm sorry you've been ill, Seamus, but I'm really glad you're getting better,' I said. 'Can I do anything for you? A cup of tea?'

'No, no, boy, just sit down and tell me what's happening in the great wide world outside this room. I'll be right and glad to get out of it again. Though mind you, Nurse Annie couldn't have been kinder to me. Thank the Lord for all our nurses, I say. What would we do here in Ardnakil without our own nurse? She's employed by the parish, privately, you know. We wouldn't have one to ourselves, otherwise, a small place like this. The government couldn't afford it.'

'I never thought about that, Seamus,' I confessed. 'But can the parish afford her?'

'People collect up for the cost regularly,' Seamus told me. 'A good friend of mine, Aidan Connelly, was great at it. He hated to miss a year. In fact, one year, when he was ill for a couple of months and then away recuperating, he was in a terrible state when he realised how little he'd collected that year.'

'Is it a story, Seamus? I'd love to hear it, but I don't want you to be tiring yourself, now.'

'I'll not do that, boy:

'Well, Aidan was at his wits' end trying to raise enough money to bring his collection up to his usual amount. He knew the parish depended on his regular contribution. He went round everyone, but over and over again their response was, 'Sure, Aidan, I've already given. I gave my usual amount to Barney (or Jimmy or Maire) – I can't squeeze out any more.'

Well, that would have been fine. As long as the money had been collected, it didn't matter to Aidan who it had gone to. There was no competition for who had collected the most – although, if there had been, Aidan would have won it regularly.

But usually, Aidan would have had a great many other gimmicks to double his amount, sponsored walks, sponsored head shaving, concerts, even car boot sales.

But he couldn't help realising time was too short for that. The parish needed to have enough money to guarantee Nurse Annie's year's salary, otherwise she would have to look for another job to keep herself alive. And they would have to know they had it by the next week.

He thought desperately about the problem, but could come up with nothing. He might be able to fit one fundraising event into the short time left, but hardly more than that. And that wouldn't be enough.

As my friends often do, he came round to me, asking for advice. But although I promised to give it my serious consideration, nothing sprang to mind. The best I was able to do was to suggest that he should widen his field of contributors, and approach people whom he didn't usually ask.

'Ah, well, Seamus, most of those would be people who've refused me in the past – that's why I don't like to ask them again,' Aidan explained.

'Sure, they might have changed their minds by now, Aidan,' I said. 'If you don't ask, you don't get, right?'

And Aidan agreed, although I could see the doubt in his eye.

So, sure enough, next day he set out to visit people he didn't know well who had never given to him before. As it turned out, I'd been right. A few of them had changed their minds, or maybe just were in a better mood, for they put something into Aidan's collection tin. But when he came to turn it out and count it later, he found that the gifts had been far from generous. He had still far too much leeway to make up.

He considered the few names remaining on his list, and sighed. One of them in particular, Miss Harmony McAndrews, filled him with, if not fear, at least a great reluctance. He well remembered his previous visit to her door, some years ago.

A hard faced, elderly woman had responded to his knock after what seemed an unnecessarily long delay.

'Well?' she snapped. 'If you're selling something, I never buy at the door.'

'I'm not selling, missus,' Aidan replied uneasily. 'I'm collecting for the village nurse, for her salary for the coming year.'

'Nonsense! If people are sick, they should go to the doctor and pay what he bills them for. I've never looked for free medical advice my whole life, and I'm not starting now.'

And with that she had shut the door in his face.

This time round, he decided to leave her until the last.

When he had covered all the people he could think of, with a certain amount of success, but with a feeling that none of them would have given particularly freely, he finally made his way to Miss Harmony McAndrews' house. It was a big house, Victorian Gothic in design, with sweeping gardens full of dark trees. Owned, surely, by someone who could afford to be generous. It might be that she would be in a better mood today.

Aidan knew very little about Miss McAndrews. He had a vague recollection that her parents had died some years ago, leaving her as their sole heir. And there had been something about the man she had been engaged to being killed in the war. In that case, maybe she was unhappy rather than bad tempered. Or perhaps, he decided realistically, she was both.

The house seemed to be in process of spring cleaning. There were piles of old broken furniture heaped in front of the garage, as if waiting for someone to take it away.

Aidan knocked at the door, but alas, his reception was even more unpleasant than the last time. Miss McAndrews was red eyed as if she had been crying, but she hardly allowed Aidan to finish his first sentence before she snapped out, 'No! I remember you, young man. I told you before that I wasn't going to encourage people to batten on others. Go away!'

Aidan went. He couldn't help feeling rather pleased at being called a young man, but he had nothing else to be pleased about. He stopped where the drive curved round out of sight of the house and counted the money in his tin. No, there was not nearly enough of it to bring his overall total to anything like previous years.

He sighed, stood up, returned the money to the tin, and prepared to go on his way, only pausing to pick up a few pieces of paper which were blowing down the drive after him. He had always been taught to pick up litter if he saw it and dispose of it later. Stuffing the papers in his pocket, he headed off home.

Later that evening he called round with me. 'It's been useless, Seamus,' he said despondently, sitting down beside me where I was basking in my garden in the last of the day's sunshine. 'We're going to be without a village nurse this year, from the look of it.'

'You never know, Aidan,' I said, hoping to cheer him up. 'Maybe something will happen, yet. Or maybe the other collectors have raised more than they usually do.'

'No, I've been inquiring into that,' Aidan said. 'None of them have even done as well as usual. I have the figures here, somewhere.'

He hoked in his pocket, brought out a handful of paper, and started sorting through it for his list.

'What's this?' he asked presently. He had an envelope in his hand, an old envelope stained with age. 'I didn't have an envelope in my pocket this morning. Where – ?' He stared at it, then his face brightened. 'I know!' he exclaimed. 'It's part of the litter I picked up in McAndrews' drive this morning.'

I took it from him and examined it. 'Yes, it's addressed to Miss Harmony McAndrews, The Turrets, Ardnakil,' I said. 'It's very old. The postmark's over sixty years ago.'

'I wonder if she meant to throw it away?' Aidan mused. 'Maybe it was in the drawer of one of those old bits of furniture she was getting rid of. I suppose I'd better return it to her, just in case. Mind you, I don't want my head bitten off again, Seamus.'

'Well, if you think she might want it, you'd be better to take it back to her,' I said firmly. 'She can't kill you, after all.'

Aidan didn't look too sure about that, but he agreed to call at The Turrets, and see if Miss McAndrews wanted the letter or not.

It was still light, a calm summer's evening, when he made his way back up the twisting drive and arrived at Miss McAndrews's front door. He knocked on it nervously, and presently the cross, elderly lady he already met twice opened it.

'You again? I don't believe it! Can you not take no for an answer, young man?' she snapped.

Before she had time to slam the door in his face, as she clearly intended to do, Aidan spoke quickly, holding out the envelope so that she could see the address. 'It's something quite different. I picked this up blowing about your drive when I was here earlier. I intended to bin it as litter, but when I looked at it, it occurred to me to wonder if you'd like it back.'

She looked at it silently for a moment, as her face changed completely. 'It's Johnnie's last letter!' she burst out at last. 'We were engaged, you know, but he was killed in the war. Come in, young man, come in. Sit down.' She took me into a large expensively furnished sitting room.

We sat opposite each other as she opened the envelope and reread the letter, which she clearly knew by heart. 'I've been crying all day because I thought I'd lost it. I've been sorting things out, getting rid of the rubbish, but of course not Johnnie's letters! I have them all. But when I read through them, I realised this one was missing. I can never thank you enough, my dear!' She sat up more firmly and wiped her eyes. 'Let me give you a glass of my father's best port,' she said. 'And of course, I'll be happy to contribute to your charity. Who do I make the cheque out to?'

And shortly afterwards Aidan, full of the best port, staggered off down the drive, holding in his hand a cheque for more than enough to pay Nurse Annie's salary for the next year without any other contributions, and an order to come back for the same again in a year's time. Leaving behind a happy, good-tempered woman whose tears had dried magically, and who had even laughed at Aidan's jokes as they shared the port together.

6 – McCool the Hero

It was a hot summer day, and I could feel the sweat beginning on my forehead as I strolled along the country lane from my little white-washed cottage to the nearby village of Ardnakil in Donegal. I had come up for a break from my busy city job to spend a relaxing few days in the cottage my grandparents left me. While there, I expected to catch up with old friends, especially my friend Seamus O'Hare, widely known as the Seanachie for his store of tales.

I'd known Seamus since I used to visit my grandparents as a child, and he'd taught me all about the country, birds and animals, flowers and trees. Besides all that, I don't think I've ever spent time with him without him telling me one of his stories – which I always enjoyed.

I was heading for T*he Golden Pheasant*, the local inn just across from the river, where there might be some fresh breezes. I was hoping to have a cooling glass of Guinness, and possibly to find old Seamus, and as I crossed the threshold into the pleasantly airy interior, I was delighted to see him sitting nursing a pint of the black stuff in the shadiest corner of all.

'Seamus, great to see you!' I greeted him, and his wrinkled, weather beaten face broke into a wide smile. He pushed his curly white hair back from his twinkling eyes and took the old pipe from his mouth.

'It's yourself, Jamie boy! Come and sit down.'

'Just as soon as I get myself something to drink, Seamus,' I said, and shortly afterwards we were sitting side by side chatting like the old friends we were.

'Such a hot day,' I said presently, and Seamus agreed.

'I hope it won't cause any fires,' he said. 'This sort of weather some-times causes outbreaks in the hills. It's a while since it's happened, mind you. You need a real heatwave, lasting some time, for that.'

'So, you've known fires break out like that, Seamus?' I asked him.

'Sure, it's happened a lot of times in my memory, boy, but not just recently. And I've known at least one fire break out when the weather was nothing special, for a quite different reason. That time, it might have been serious, but as it happened, things worked out okay.'

'Tell me the story, Seamus.'

'I will, Jamie, I will.' Seamus settled himself more comfortably, took another sip from his glass, and began:

'My friend Lizzie MacPherson was a good woman, but she had her funny wee quirks, like most of us. Lizzie lived on the outskirts of Ardnakil, with her husband Joe. They ran a farm, and did well enough, though it was hard work, as most farms are. There was only one thing missing in Joe's and Lizzie's life, and that was a child of their own, or maybe more than one. She and Joe had been married for over five years before Lizzie finally fell pregnant, to their great delight.

The baby was a fine sturdy boy, and they called him Steven, after Joe's father. They had great hopes for him as someone to take over the farm in due course when he was grown and they were no longer so capable. By the time he was eight, Stevie was already showing all the signs of being a farmer's son. He loved the farm and the animals, and had great fun helping with the harvest.

There was only one problem. Stevie wanted a dog of his own, and that was where Lizzie's quirks came in. She had been bitten by a dog when she was even younger than Stevie, and it had left her with a lasting dread of them. She could just about accept the farm dogs, which she knew were needed, and which never came near the farmhouse, but the idea of a pet dog in the house was unthinkable to her. When Stevie put in his request, she put her foot down firmly.

'I'm having no dog in this house, boy,' she said. 'So just get that into your head and keep it there.' She was a strong willed woman, and Stevie knew there was no moving her when once she'd made her mind up. But Stevie for all his youth was strong minded too, and he at once began making plans.

His friend Jenny Thompson who lived not far away had a female dog who had recently had a litter of puppies, and Jenny had offered Stevie his pick of them. Stevie was overjoyed, and when he went round secretly to inspect the wriggling basketful, he fell in love at once with a little black and white creature with a black patch over one eye.

Hugging the puppy to him as if he would never let it go, he stammered out, 'Aw, Jenny, can I really have him? I can't believe it!'

'Sure, we'll be glad to give him to you, Stevie,' Jenny replied, 'for we can't keep them all, much as I'd love to. We're giving them away to anyone we can trust to look after them properly.'

'I'll do that, Jenny, for sure.'

Stevie, cuddling the new puppy under his jacket, ran home. But as he approached the farm, he slowed down. He wouldn't be allowed to bring McCool, as he'd decided to call him, into his house. Where, then, could he keep him? It didn't take him long to decide. There was a huge barn not too near the house, with a warm dry hayloft above it. Stevie climbed the ladder – no easy job with McCool to hold on to – and inspected it. He would have to rig up some sort of kennel type affair to keep McCool from roaming – he already looked as adventurous as his namesake – or even from falling through the opening where the ladder reached, and getting badly hurt.

Stevie spent the rest of the afternoon seeking out wooden planks and wire netting, and presently he had set up the necessary enclosure, not too small, because he didn't want McCool to feel trapped and imprisoned. He hunted around the farm outbuildings and found a couple of dishes not currently in use, that he could put food and water in. He made a rough and ready collar and lead for the puppy. Then bursting with joy and pride, he brought McCool round to show him off to me.

Like Stevie, I fell in love with the wriggly black and white puppy straightaway. But I knew there was trouble coming.

'Where are you planning to keep him, Stevie? And how will you feed him?'

'In the hayloft. I've built a house for him,' Stevie told me proudly. 'So he won't fall down the opening. And I'll take enough food for him from the kitchen.'

'Your mammy will be bound to notice before long, Stevie boy.'

'Well, I suppose they'll have to know sooner or later,' Stevie admitted. 'I can't hide him forever. But I want to have him for a while at least, in case I can't get them to agree to keep him.'

His face fell at the thought. He was only a very little boy, after all. I could see that he was struggling not to cry at the idea of losing McCool.

I felt desperately sorry for him, but had nothing much to suggest. 'If they tell you you can't keep him, you could always bring him round to me and I'd look after him. You could come and play with him and take him for walks as often as you wanted. I know it wouldn't be like having him at home, but maybe better than nothing?'

'Thanks, Seamus. You're awful kind.' But I could see that he knew it wouldn't be a real solution.

I gave some thought to the problem over the next week or so, but came up with nothing better.

One sunny afternoon I strolled round to the MacPhersons' farm and wandered over to the barn with the hayloft. I wanted to have another look at McCool, and to see if Stevie was still managing to keep him a secret. But there was no sign of either of them around. Finally I gave up and went for a walk in the fields, where I passed a happy, drowsy afternoon lying back in the long grass, listening to the lark song and seeing how many types of bird I could spot.

The sun was still bright when I made my way back to the hayloft again.

'Stevie? Are you there?' I called up. There was no answer.

Then, to my dismay, I saw Lizzie McPherson coming hurrying towards me. I moved hastily away from the hayloft, and Lizzie stopped to speak to me at what I hoped was a reasonable distance.

'Seamus, am I glad to see you! Listen here, have you seen wee Stevie? He went out before his lunch time and he hasn't been back since, and his tea's ready now. It's not like him, so it's not. He's got me all worried.'

'Och, Lizzie, he'll be okay. He'll have gone off trying to catch fish or something and forgotten the time. I'll keep an eye out for him, and chase him home when I find him.'

Lizzie's face cleared a bit, but she was still upset. 'Seamus, that'd be great. You're a real friend. But supposing you don't see him?'

'Sure, he'll turn up sooner or later, Lizzie. Have you any reason to think he won't?'

And at that, Lizzie burst into tears. I did my best to soothe her, and led her over to a block of wood where she and I could sit down and talk.

'Seamus, it's all my fault. I think maybe he's run away, and the dear knows what'll happen to him.'

'Why should it be your fault, Lizzie?'

'He was asking me again if he could keep a dog in the house. It seems Jenny down the road has some puppies and she's offered him one. But, Seamus, I hate the idea of a dog in the house, you know that, and I told him so. And if he's run away, because I've been hard on him – och, Seamus, what'll I do?'

'He'll turn up, Lizzie. And maybe,' I added drily, 'you might change your mind about the dog. A harmless wee puppy who grows up knowing the people in the house isn't going to turn on any of them, now is he?'

Lizzie said nothing, just burst out crying again. It was then that we both heard it. A puppy's shrill yelps, loud and piercing.

Lizzie stopped crying and we stared at each other. At the same moment, we both smelled a whiff of burning wood and hay, and it was coming from the barn.

At the time we didn't know it, but Stevie had cried himself to sleep in the hayloft, cuddling McCool to him. Before that, he had opened the loft's wide upper door to let the fresh air in. He hadn't noticed, as he nodded over to sleep, that the sun was shining in directly through that open door, down onto the empty lemonade bottle Stevie had brought with him, and had drunk up and cast aside.

But McCool, who hadn't slept, noticed it. And he noticed that the beams of sunlight had struck a light through the glass bottle onto the hay piled all around, and had started, at first gently, but then more fiercely, a fire which was rapidly spreading all through the loft.

As one, Lizzie and I ran towards the smoke, and as we came nearer we could hear the crackling sound of the burning hay.

We burst in through the door of the barn, and we both saw McCool, his black and white face peering over the edge of the opening where the ladder was perched, and his barks coming furiously. A moment later, we saw Stevie, one leg stretching down to the ladder, and his hand reaching out to seize McCool and carry him to safety.

I rushed forward and took McCool from Stevie's arms as he reached him down to me, then Lizzie was beside me, helping Stevie to the ground.

There was no time for anything except escape from the barn, but as soon as the boy and his dog were safe, Lizzie and I set about pouring buckets of water over the flames, until we were sure it was completely out. Thanks to McCool's barking, we'd got there soon enough to tackle the fire before it spread too much.

'McCool's a hero, mammy,' Stevie said. He could see it was the right moment. 'If he hadn't woken me up, I'd have been trapped in the fire. Please may I keep him?'

Lizzie, torn between tears and thankfulness, could only say, 'Of course you can, darlin'. Sure, wasn't he sent by the Lord above to save your life?' She threw her arms round Stevie and McCool, hugging them.

I've never seen such an ecstatic face as Stevie's right then – and Lizzie, her son safe from the fire, looked pretty delighted, too!

7 – Tommy and the Wandering Hen

The first spring flowers were out, colouring the meadows and road-sides with the white of snowdrops and the gold, white, and pale and dark purple of crocuses. The air was crisp and bright, and the pale winter sky was being coaxed to a deeper blue by the kindness of the sun, stroking it with gentle hands. I strolled through the fields, taking care to keep clear of the new green shoots of barley and oats, walking only on the tracks at the edge of each field – I didn't want to bring down the wrath of any local farmer on me. The day was exhilarating, and as I went along I found myself singing happily.

I had come up to spend a long weekend in the little whitewashed cottage I'd inherited from my grandparents, in the small village of Ardnakil in Donegal. I always enjoyed getting away there from my busy city job, and meeting up with old friends, particularly my friend old Seamus O'Hare, that fount of knowledge about the countryside, with his seemingly endless store of tales of the past.

As I had hoped, Seamus was also out, enjoying the fresh spring day, and it wasn't long before I saw him sauntering along at the edge of a nearby field, his hands in his pockets, his disreputable old hat pushed back on his curly white hair, his lips above the white beard pursed into a whistle. When he saw me, he waved and called out, and we hurried to meet each other.

'Isn't it a wonderful day, boy?' exclaimed Seamus, beaming all over his wrinkled, weather beaten old face. 'It's good to see you here again. Glad to see you keeping to the edge of the fields, too!'

'Why, you taught me that yourself, Seamus, when I was the size of sixpence and used to visit my grandparents' cottage. One of the many things you taught me about the country.'

We were strolling along together by now, for lovely day though it was, there was too sharp a nip in the air to encourage us to stand still.

'Oh there's nothing that annoys a farmer more than seeing people carelessly trampling down his growing crops,' Seamus said. 'I knew one, in particular, Tommy Harrison, who used to fly right off the handle when he saw it happening.'

'I'm not surprised, Seamus,' I said.

'Mind you, there was one time, when Tommy's crops had been especially badly damaged and he was particularly angry, that it all worked out for the best for him.'

'This sounds like the start of a story, Seamus,' I laughed. 'Are you going to tell me how it goes?'

'If you want, boy. But maybe we should head for my cottage – it's not far from here, as you know. And we'll have some tea to warm us up, before I go on with the story.'

Ten minutes later, we were sitting comfortably beside Seamus's glowing turf fire, each with a welcome cup of hot tea in our hands, and Seamus sighed with pleasure and said, 'Nothing like a cup of tea by a turf fire, is there, Jamie?'

'Nothing. And one of your stories will make it even better, Seamus.'

Seamus smiled, and began:

'This is a story about my friend, Tommy Harrison, as I told you. I'd known Tommy since we were at the village school, so that's a while ago. At the time I'm talking about, we were both in our twenties, and Tommy was running the family farm, his parents having died. Tommy was even more protective of his young plants than most. Maybe it was his red hair that made him fly off the handle so easily. He was a big, lumbering sort of fella, clumsy, but good looking for all that, with this thatch of red hair that could be seen for miles around.

As he told me later, there was something or someone – more likely an animal – trampling down and tearing up his newly growing barley, and Tommy was determined to find out who or what it was, and put a stop to it. So he began, in whatever time he could spare, to lurk about, as much out of sight as he could manage, near the field where the worst damage was being done, and after a day or two his patience was rewarded. As he kept a keen watch over the field he noticed a ripple of movement running along through the shoots. Convinced that this must be the guilty party, he crept cautiously up, and when he felt he was near enough he sprang out at the source of the movement, his arms spread to catch it.

There was a loud squawk, a ruffle of feathers, and Tommy found himself clutching a large hen.

Not for long, though. As he tried to get a better grip on the fowl, it somehow slipped from his fingers and scuttled off, in a half running, half hopping manner, even attempting, not very successfully, to fly, across Tommy's barley field. Tommy dived after it, his temper taking over so that he forgot to consider where he was planting his own large feet.

With no thought of the damage he was doing, he chased that bird round and across and back. It was a quick mover, he had to give it that. Although Tommy nearly had it more than once, it kept evading his grasp. Tommy stopped occasionally to draw breath and wipe the sweat from his forehead, and once, looking round, he noticed in horror the further damage that he and the hen between them were doing to his field. But he was determined not to give up.

Finally with a squawk of triumph and what Tommy was convinced was a wicked gleam of victory in her eye, the hen (Tommy had begun to call her in his own mind the Wicked Witch of the West) wriggled successfully through a gap in the hedge, which was presumably not only her exit but her original means of entrance. Tommy, throwing all caution to the winds, forced his way after her.

He was in time to see her making her way with a fresh turn of speed across that field and towards the fence which was the boundary between his own land and that of his neighbour. By this time Tommy was determined not to be beaten. Running with renewed vigour, he caught up with the Wicked Witch just as she squeezed through a narrow opening between two planks of the fence. Tommy scrambled over the fence after her, landed almost on top of the bird, and managed at last to grab her successfully. Then, a grin of triumph on his face, he strode off towards the farmhouse to make his complaints.

As he approached the white two storey building, he tried to remember what he knew of its owners.

Their name, he thought he'd heard, was Dougan, and they were newcomers to the district, having bought the farm from its previous owners, an elderly couple who had given up farming and retired.

He had probably heard more about them, but for the life of him he couldn't remember anything. Tommy had developed a bad habit of ignoring everyone around him since he taken over the family farm and thrown himself heart and soul into making it a success.

As he strode up to the house, his grip on the Wicked Witch firm, and a scowl of anger on his face, a man came round one corner of the building and came over to him, smiling.

'Hullo!' he said. 'You must be our next door neighbour, Tommy Harrison, right? I've heard a lot about you. I'm Fran Dougan. Been meaning to call round, but you know how it is – busy, busy, busy. Nice to meet you.' He held out his hand to shake Tommy's.

Tommy ignored him.

'Is this your hen?' he demanded in a voice like thunder.

'Oh, not mine. Rosie takes to do with the hens – I know nothing about them – and don't want to, either. Rosie!' he called.

A sweet voice answered, 'Coming!' and a girl came round the house from the other direction.

Tommy's mouth dropped open. He felt the ground give way under his feet. He was looking at the sweetest face he'd ever seen, with eyes a lovely sparkling hazel, lips soft and beautiful as rose petals, and an innocent, welcoming smile.

'Oh, you've found Sophie!' she exclaimed in a delighted voice. 'How kind of you to bring her back!'

'This is Tommy Harrison, Rosie, from the farm next to ours,' Fran Dougan put in.

'Tommy, thank you so much. I'm afraid she's got into the habit of getting through your fence and escaping.'

Tommy, all thoughts of his damaged crops vanished, thrust the Wicked Witch, or rather Sophie, into Rosie's arms, and found himself stammering out an apology for the gap in his fence and promising to fix it straight away.

'That's lovely of you, Tommy!' Rosie Dougan beamed. 'And you must come to tea with us when you're finished. We want to get to know our nearest neighbour.'

So a couple of hours later, the gap in the fence fixed, Tommy found himself sitting down to eat with the Dougans and enjoying Rosie's excellent cooking, though with little enough appetite. He remarked on the tenderness of the beef and the lightness of the pastry, and saw Rosie's face blush with delight.

'Yes, I'm a lucky man to have someone like Rosie to cook for me,' Fran said, smiling. 'Don't you think so, Tommy?'

Tommy did. When he got up from the table presently and made his farewells, he was hard put to it to keep his depression from showing.

I ran into him later that evening. It was growing dark, and I almost bumped into Tommy as he hung silently over the millpond.

'Tommy!' I exclaimed. 'What are you up to? If you don't look out, you'll be over the edge.'

'That might be the best thing for me, Seamus,' Tommy said. 'I don't think my life's worth living any more.'

I tut-tutted and patted him on the shoulder. 'Come on home with me, Tommy. I'll make you a cup of tea and you can tell me all about it.' And I led him away from the dark, gloomy pool with its dangerously tempting depths.

I took him to my cottage and we sat, just as you and I are doing now, drinking tea beside a warm turf fire, and after some friendly chat, Tommy began to tell me his troubles.

'I met a girl today, Seamus. The loveliest, sweetest girl I've ever seen. I love her, Seamus. I'll never stop loving her. But Seamus, she's already married. And her husband's a nice fella, as far as I can see. She seems very happy with him. There's nothing I can do about it, I know that. I'm so unhappy, Seamus. If I'd jumped in the millpond and drowned tonight like I wanted to, I'd have been better off. I can't live with this pain and misery.'

I tried to tell him that many of us had felt like that, and got over it. I had myself, although like Tommy I was still a young man. But I could see that he didn't believe me. Presently it occurred to me to ask who this girl was.

'Her name is Rosie Dougan,' Tommy said. 'If only it could be Rosie Harrison, Seamus, I'd be such a happy man. She and her husband Fran have just recently moved into the farm beside me – so to make matters worse I'll be seeing her all the time. Maybe I should sell up and go to Australia.'

I found it hard not to burst out laughing, but I controlled myself for fear of upsetting Tommy even more.

'I've a bit of news for you, Tommy,' I said with a face as grave as I could make it.

'Oh?' Tommy sounded far from interested.

'I met your new friends the Dougans out walking recently, Tommy.'

'Oh?' Tommy sounded slightly more interested. 'So you see what I mean about Rosie, then. Isn't she the most beautiful girl ever, Seamus? So gentle and kind.'

'Sure, she's a good looking wee girl all right, Tommy.'

Tommy gave a heartrending sigh. I hastened to put him out of his misery. 'Did you notice her left hand, Tommy?'

'Her left hand?'

I couldn't hold back any longer.

'No wedding ring, boyo!'

'What?' Tommy gaped at me, not quite understanding yet.

'If you hadn't jumped to conclusions, you great eedjit, you'd have found out, like me, that Rosie and Fran Dougan are brother and sister, not husband and wife!'

Tommy's face was a picture. He jumped up, and was for racing round to see Rosie straightaway, until I pointed out the time. 'She'll be in bed sleeping now. But you could go round at a reasonable hour tomorrow, and start your courting.'

And so he did. And not many months later, to my delight as well as Tommy's, Rosie Dougan did indeed become Mrs Rosie Harrison.

8 – Seamus and the Horse Trader

Today the sun had some real warmth in it, and I was enjoying my walk in the fresh air. I had come up to the little Donegal village of Ardnakil to stay in the small whitewashed cottage left to me by my grandparents. The lanes were a marvellous contrast to the busy city where I lived and worked.

Presently I came into the village street, and as I walked I noticed a poster advertising a coming horse fair. I was intrigued. In all the years I'd been coming to Ardnakil, I never remembered hearing of a horse fair there. I made a mental note to ask my old friend Seamus O'Hare about it whenever I bumped into him. And just as I thought this, who should come ambling along the village street but Seamus, his disreputable old hat on his curly white hair, a merry twinkle lighting up the mischievous eyes in his wrinkled weather-beaten face, and a welcoming smile on his lips.

'Jamie, boy, it's yourself!'

I'd known Seamus since I came up to visit my grandparents as a child, and through the long lazy days he had taught me everything there was to know about the countryside of Donegal, its birds and plants and animals. Besides this, he'd told me innumerable stories about himself and his friends and acquaintances, and the habit had persisted, for Seamus was a real *Seanachie*, which is Irish for storyteller, and I always enjoyed his tales, whether funny or sad.

When our friendly greetings were over, I remembered to ask him about the horse fair I'd seen advertised.

'I didn't know they had horse fairs here, Seamus?' I asked. 'Isn't it too small a village for such a thing?'

'Oh, I don't know about that,' said Seamus. 'We have a lot of people round here with an interest in horses. There's Mr Brendan McGarvey, for instance, who has the big stable out yonder and runs his horses in all the important races. Then there's Daniel and Amy O'Flynn (who used to be Amy Cadogan) of Five Trees Farm. And a whole clatter of others, farmers and the like, who own a horse or two. Then there's the folks who come for miles around, looking to drive a good bargain.'

'Horse trading has a bad name, hasn't it?' I asked. 'A lot of cheating goes on, I've heard.'

'Ah, well, I wouldn't say it was as bad as that. Some cheating, surely. But not really a lot. A few bad apples in the barrel, like you always get. There was Jackie O'Brien, now. He was a bad rascal and no mistake. Cheated a friend of mine, wee Davie Harrison, a fair number of years ago now.'

'Is it a story, Seamus? Are you going to tell me about it?'

'I'll do that, boy. But first of all, let's go into *The Golden Pheasant* and settle ourselves down comfortably with a pint of the black stuff, if that suits you.'

It suited me very nicely, and a few minutes later we were sitting in the warm snug with a table between us on which rested two full glasses. Seamus began his story:

'Davie Harrison was a good friend of mine, although he was a fair bit older. At the time I'm telling you about he was coming up to fifty, and I'd have been somewhere in my twenties. Davie was very happily married to a sweet woman of the name of Martha, and the only fly in the ointment was Martha's poor health. She had been suffering from bronchial trouble for some years and it didn't seem to go away.

Davie talked to me about it often. He would call round to the cottage and sit chatting and Martha's bad health would always came up after a while. One particular evening, he had been telling me that they would be married twenty-five years in four more weeks. 'Our silver wedding anniversary, Seamus,' Davie said. 'Hard to believe! I'm planning to take her away for a bit of a break, just to celebrate. I've been saving up for months. She doesn't know, I've been keeping it a surprise. I think the rest and the sea air ought to perk her up a bit.'

Davie and Martha ran a general store in the village in those days, and did well enough, but I knew fine well that they didn't do much more than scrape by.

Chapter 8 – Seamus and the Horse Trader

'I haven't been able to save all that much, of course,' Davie went on. 'About fifty pounds. But it'll give us a week in Bundoran, at any rate.'

Fifty pounds was worth more those days, but still wasn't enough for a better holiday than Davie was planning. Still, I was surprised he had managed to save so much.

'Good for you, Davie,' I said, and we left it at that.

It was a couple of weeks later when the horse fair came to Ardnakil, and Jackie O'Brien took advantage of Davie's innocence on the subject of horses. I wasn't with Davie or I would have warned him at the time, but I heard about it afterwards.

It seems that Davie was strolling along in the direction of the fair when he bumped into Jackie O'Brien. He was looking a bit down in the mouth and was leading a brown horse. The creature had dull, dry looking brown hair and didn't look up to much.

'Davie Harrison,' said Jackie O'Brien. 'I'm glad to see you. Are you heading for the horse fair?'

'I am that, Jackie,' Davie answered.

'So am I. But I can't really afford the time. My old mother's been taken sick, and I need to get the doctor for her. I don't know what to do. This mare is so special that Mr Brendan McGarvey told me he'll pay five thousand pounds for her if I bring her along today. But to tell you the truth, if I could find someone to take her off my hands for a little as a hundred pounds, I'd hand her over gladly, and save myself the time. I'm so worried about my poor old mother.'

Davie's soft heart was touched. 'Och, I'm right and sorry to hear that, Jackie,' he said. 'I wish I could help.'

Jackie gave him a look. 'Well, maybe you can, Davie. If you'd like to make a bit of money yourself, that is?'

Now, with Martha's holiday coming up so soon, a bit of extra money was just what Davie wanted. 'What do you mean, Jackie?' he asked.

'Why, if you felt like taking this fine mare off my hands, you could bring her along to Mr Brendan McGarvey at the fair, and collect that five thousand pounds he promised me. I won't ask you for a penny of it! That is, if you've got a hundred pounds to buy her from me. I couldn't afford to let her go for less.'

Davie's face fell. 'A hundred pounds? That's a sum of money I've never seen all at one time, Jackie. The most I have is fifty.'

'That's too bad, Davie.' Jackie was silent for a moment. Then he spoke. 'I'll do it!' he exclaimed. 'I like you, Davie, and I'd like to put some good your way. And I can't waste any more time. I need to get away and fetch the doctor. So I'll take your fifty pounds, although it's cheating myself I am, for sure. Have you got it there?'

Davie had. He wasn't too sure about the whole business, but Jackie seemed so pleased to be doing him a favour, and at the same time so worried about his mother, that he made up his mind.

'Done, Jackie.' He fished in his pocket. 'Here's the fifty pounds.'

'And here's the finest mare in the country,' said Jackie O'Brien. He handed Davie the bridle. 'I'd better be off now. You've done me a good turn, Davie, but I'm glad to think I've done one for you as well.' He slapped the mare on the flanks, stared for a moment at his hand and rubbed it unobtrusively on his trouser leg, and made off hastily along the road in the opposite direction to the horse fair.

Davie walked on towards the fair, leading his new purchase. His mind was full of roseate dreams. He would be able to give Martha the holiday of a lifetime, and still have lots of money left, to use in other ways to bring her to better health. A more expensive doctor, perhaps. Although when he thought of it, it would be hard to get any doctor kinder and wiser than Doctor McGrath, who'd been looking after Martha for years. Ah, well, he'd think of something.

The horse fair loomed near, and he went in search of Mr Brendan McGarvey. He had a quick look at the mare first. His original bad opinion of her struck him again. Her coat was so dull, it made her look in bad health. Still, if someone like Mr Brendan McGarvey, known all over the country for his expertise with horses, thought her 'the finest mare in the country,' who was Davie to question him?

Mr Brendan McGarvey's voice could be heard booming out across the fair ground, driving a hard bargain for one of his horses. Davie stood meekly in the background until the sale was completed, then he led the mare forward.

'This is the mare you wanted to buy from Jackie O'Brien, Mr McGarvey,' he said proudly. 'He says you're offering five thousand for her. She belongs to me now, Jackie sold her to me. And I'd be happy to sell her on to you for the same price you offered Jackie.'

For a moment Mr Brendan McGarvey stared at Davie in amazement. Then he burst into a loud roar of laughter which turned all heads in his direction. 'Me give five thousand pounds for that bag of bones? Are you telling me you let Jackie O'Brien swindle you out of real money for that animal? Why, I wouldn't give five thousand pence for her, or even five pence. A fool and his money are soon parted, Davie Harrison. Now take her away out of my sight before you scare off all my costumers!'

Davie couldn't believe his ears. What was he to do now? He'd spent Martha's holiday money on a mare that was worth nothing. He was turning sadly away when I caught up with him. The loud laughter had attracted my attention, along with everyone else at the fair.

'What's going on, Davie?'

It didn't take long for Davie to tell me his story. My first reaction was anger against that swindler Jackie O'Brien. 'If only I'd been there to warn you not to trust a man with such a reputation as a cheat! He's one of the chief reasons horse trading has such a bad name!' I burst out.

'Seamus, what am I going to do now?'

The sight of Davie's woebegone face pulled me out of my anger. Instead, I began to think. First of all, I had a good look at the mare, and began to wonder where Jackie O'Brien had got her. I patted her soothingly, for the laughter and general confusion seemed to have upset her. Then, as I took my hand away and the palm of it caught my eye, something occurred to me. I remembered something Amy O'Flynn had told me earlier.

'Davie, let's take this mare into one of the stalls and wash her down.'

Amy O'Flynn willingly allowed us to use one of her temporary stalls. We worked hard at the mare, washing off the brown dye and revealing a glossy white coat underneath.

'Amy,' I called over to her. 'What was the name of that mare you told me was stolen from you?'

Amy came towards us. 'White Fire,' she said.

At the sound of her name, the mare lifted up her head and gave a joyful whinny.

Amy seized Davie by both hands and exclaimed, 'It's White Fire! It must have been Jackie O'Brien who stole her! I've been worried sick. She's one of our best racers – Daniel and I have been looking forward to winning thousands on her this coming season. Davie, how can I ever thank you enough for bringing her back?'

I saw Davie was at a loss for words, so I spoke up firmly. 'You could pay him back the fifty pounds he gave that Jackie O'Brien for her. And I think you might like to double it to reward him for finding your valuable mare, Amy.'

'Of course I will,' Amy said happily. 'And what's more, I'll not only double it, I'll multiply it by ten. Is five hundred pounds any good to you, Davie?'

Davie could only look at her with his jaw hanging open.

Amy was as good as her word. She gave Davie the five hundred pounds straightaway. So, in spite of Jackie O'Brien's tricks, White Fire won race after race that season, and Davie was able to give Martha the best holiday of her life after all.

9 – Seamus and the Medicine Man

It was the height of summer and the weather was lovely for once. The sun was scorching down, the sky was a beautiful bright blue with a few fluffy white clouds, and we hadn't seen a drop of rain for over a week. It was a heat wave, and while it was, if anything, too hot in the middle of the city where I worked, here in the small Donegal village of Ardnakil, where I had come for a short break, it was perfect.

I was tempted to spend the afternoon lounging in the shade of the huge chestnut tree in the garden of the small whitewashed cottage I had inherited from my grandparents, sipping a long drink and reading, but after a few hours I decided to take a stroll towards the river in search of a cooling breeze.

I hadn't gone far along the river bank when I met my old friend Seamus O'Hare, lying on the bank with his eyes closed, chewing at a piece of grass. I've known Seamus since I came up as a child to stay with my grandparents and Seamus had told me all about country life, the animals, insects, plants and flowers. Seamus was a bit of a rascal, a poacher with little regard for the law, but he overflowed with kindness to his many friends.

'Seamus!' I called. 'Good to see you!'

Seamus opened his eyes, took the grass from between his lips, and gave me his usual cheery grin, his eyes twinkling as he pushed back the disreputable old cap from his curly white hair.

'The same to yourself, boy. What a day! Couldn't beat it with a big stick.'

I settled myself comfortably on the bank beside him, and said, 'So how are things with you, Seamus? You're enjoying this weather?'

'Couldn't be better, boy. It reminds me of a spell of great weather we had many years ago, when I was about the age you were yourself when I first met you. We had a travelling fair stopping just outside the village at that time – I well remember it, and the problems it caused for my friend Jenny Doyle.'

'So, is there a story about Jenny for you to tell me, Seamus?'

'Indeed there is,' Seamus said:

'Jenny was older than me, a widow with a son about ten called Donal, who was a friend of mine, although a bit younger. Donal was a bright lad, but his health wasn't as good as it might be. He suffered from chronic diabetes, and I knew the cost of his medicine kept Jenny pretty hard up – not that she grudged a penny of it. A large part of what she earned by cleaning for some of the people in the big houses round about – such as the Honourable Marjorie, and Lord Kilmarnock – went on Donal's insulin.

Hard up or not, Jenny was a generous woman and had always been very kind to me, inviting me in for the odd cup of tea and fresh baked soda bread with lashings of butter. She even gave me a bowl of Irish stew occasionally, and I can tell you it was all more than welcome to me, for that was the time when my father had left home to work on the railways and ended up dead in an accident. I had to fend for myself from then on, and although I could feed myself by tickling fish and picking wild mushrooms and suchlike, anything extra was much appreciated.

Jenny used to talk to me as if I was a friend of her own age. I suppose she didn't have too many other friends, for she was a newcomer to Ardnakil, and her husband had died not long after they'd settled here. She was a great one for unconventional medicines, liked to make her own nettle tea, for instance, and recommended various herbs for coughs and other things. She never pushed them on me, but enjoyed telling me about her latest discoveries. As far as I could see, she was doing no one any harm by her unusual medicines, and I just smiled and said how interesting it was. And indeed it was, and nowadays there are thousands of people who would agree with her.

But when the travelling fair arrived, it was a different matter.

One of the various sideshows at the fair was a tent labelled, *'The Amazing Alphonso, Medicine Man.'* There was a poster outside, with a picture of a silver haired man with flowing moustaches, and *'Doctor Alphonso's wonderful medicines will cure all your aches and pains and diseases. Come inside and buy whatever you need!'*

When I dropped in to see Jenny not long after the fair had come, she was bubbling over with excitement about 'Doctor' Alphonso and his wonderful cures for everything. Well, it still seemed harmless enough to me, so long as she didn't waste too much of her scanty income on a swindler – if he was one. I didn't know anything about the man, but I reckoned I might try to find out. I owed Jenny whatever help I could give her.

I went along to see the Amazing Alphonso that same evening, and for sure he put on an impressive show. There was a crowd clustered round his tent, and he had a table set up inside it with bottles and tins of ointment spread out. He talked strikingly for a short time about each of his medicines in turn, and then offered that particular bottle for sale.

When he saw that he had sold as many as he could of that one, he moved on to the next and talked in the same stirring way about it, before selling it in its turn. The illnesses these goods were supposed to cure would have filled a medical dictionary, and Alphonso's long words and technical language convinced his audience that he was a wise, clever man who knew all about his subject.

It didn't convince me, however, for I had noticed that a young friend of mine, Ginger Bailey, was working as his assistant, handing out the bottles and taking the money, and I knew that Ginger was a lad I would trust as far as I could throw him.

I hung around until the good doctor decided to shut up shop for the time being. 'That's all for now, folks,' he boomed in his most imposing voice. 'But I'll be back to bring you everything you need for your various illnesses this time tomorrow.'

Leaving Ginger to put the goods away inside the tent, he strolled about chatting to his customers. Presently, he would head for *The Golden Pheasant*, where, I was told later, he regularly drank plenty and talked even more, about his wonderful cures, drumming up interest for next day.

I decided to give Ginger a hand with the bottles and tins of ointment. He was grateful for the help, and as we put things away, we talked.

'How did you get into this, Ginger?' I asked him.

'Just luck, Seamus. I was hanging round the fair, having a go at the roll a penny, when yer man Alphonso came past and said, 'Hey, boy, want to earn a few quid?' I said yes, and next thing you know I'm working for him.'

'And you like it?'

'Yeah, it's dead easy.' Ginger looked as if he might be going to say a bit more, but just then we heard Alphonso's voice calling out, 'Hey, boy, aren't you finished yet? I want to get away. I've got your week's wages here for you.' And Ginger scuttled out to see his boss, hardly bothering to thank me for my help or say goodbye.

I took myself off after that, meaning to call round with Jenny the next day and try to discourage her before she bought any more of the Amazing Alphonso's rubbish. But alas, when I got there, it was already too late.

'Seamus, come away in,' she greeted me. 'Look what I've got here!' She flourished a large bottle full of a greeny yellow mixture. 'I ran into the Amazing Alphonso this morning in the village, and got talking to him, and he told me he had just the thing for Donal. It will save him having to depend on that expensive insulin he takes. Alphonso says this is just as good – and half the price!'

I was only a young fella, but I knew enough to see that what Jenny was planning would be very dangerous. If the doctor had said that Donal needed insulin regularly, then he knew what he was talking about. Stopping Donal from taking it and giving him something the Great Alphonso had dreamed up might well be disastrous.

But Jenny didn't listen to me. And I could hardly blame her, for kind as she was, she thought of me as not much more than a child. I needed something to convince her in time, before she got started on the substitution. She still had enough insulin left for the rest of the week, she told me, and after that she wouldn't have to buy any more.

I went home and gave the matter a great deal of serious thought.

Next evening I made my way round to the Amazing Alphonso's tent, and when he had finished I helped Ginger again. Since he wasn't due any more wages he was in no hurry. We got chatting again, and this time he told me some interesting things which I hoped I could use.

'Would you like to come round and meet my friend Jenny Doyle tomorrow, Ginger?' I asked him. 'She's a good customer of your boss Alphonso, and she'd love to meet you. She makes great soda bread and I'm sure she'd give you some warm from the griddle, and a hot cup of tea, if you'd like it.'

Chapter 9 – Seamus and the Medicine Man

Well, as I'd known he would, Ginger, who wasn't well paid, jumped at the chance of some free food, and I could see he was also happy to have the chance to show off about his knowledge of Alphonso and his medicines. Ginger wasn't the brightest of boys, and I was hoping I could get him to give himself – and Alphonso – away. We walked round to Jenny's cottage next morning, and on the way I encouraged him to tell me more about his work for Alphonso.

'Jenny would love to hear all this, Ginger,' I said, and I saw Ginger was swallowing what I said.

When we reached the cottage, Jenny had just finished baking, and as usual offered us tea and soda bread.

As we sat enjoying it, I explained that Ginger worked for the Amazing Alphonso. Jenny was very interested.

'Tell Jenny some of the things you've been telling me, Ginger,' I encouraged him, and straightaway he began repeating some of what he'd told me already. He was boasting about his knowledge and skill, enjoying showing-off, and didn't notice Jenny's reactions.

'I know a lot about it by now,' he said. 'Alphonso's been showing me how to make up the medicines, so one of these days I'm going to set up for myself and go round the fairs – the Great Doctor Bailieo – what d'ye think of that, eh?'

'So how do you make them, Ginger?' I prompted him.

'Mostly salt and water,' Ginger told us with a knowing wink. 'But you add a wee bit of various flowers to colour it. Whin blossom for the yellow coloured bottles, rose petals for the pink stuff, and like that. Easy-peasy! It costs next to nothing to make – the bottles and labels are the only bits of it that take money. And we sell them for ten times what we spend on them.'

'So,' Jenny said slowly, 'this bottle I have here' – she produced the greeny yellow mixture she had shown me previously – 'what would be in this, then?'

'Oh, that one has leaves and some whin blossom. Comes out a good colour, doesn't it? And of course, mostly salt and water, like I said.'

Jenny's face was a picture. She drew herself together, but before she could throw the bottle at Ginger's head, as she showed every sign of doing, it dawned on Ginger that his words hadn't been received with the admiration he'd expected. Next moment he was out of the door like a rocket and running for his life.

Jenny just stood there, looking as if she didn't know whether to laugh or cry.

'D'you want to come round with me tonight to tell the Amazing Alphonso, in front of all his customers, that you want your money back, because you can mix up salt and water for yourself, Jenny?' I suggested. 'I should think that might put an end to his little game.'

Jenny jumped at the idea. 'I'll be saying a lot more than that, Seamus, if I once get started!' she said enthusiastically.

And sure enough, after what Jenny had to say that night, the Amazing Alphonso packed his bags, and was never seen again at any fair in Ardnakil.

10 – Flying Flynn

I had snatched a few summer days' break from my busy city job to escape the stifling heat. As I strolled through the fields near the small whitewashed cottage at Ardnakil left to me by my grandparents, enjoying the gentle breeze, I heard someone whistling. The whistler broke into song, and presently I could hear the words.

> *And one of the gentlemen gave a 'Ha! Ha!*
> *'Is that the great dog you call Master McGrath?'*

It was my old friend Seamus O'Hare. I'd known Seamus since I came up as a child to visit my grandparents, and he taught me all about the countryside, birds, animals, trees and flowers.

I listened to a couple more verses:

> *Lord Lurgan stepped forward and said, 'Gentlemen,*
> *If there's any among you has money to spend –*
> *For your grand English nobles I don't care a straw –*
> *Here's five thousand to one upon Master McGrath.'*
>
> *McGrath he looked up and he wagged his old tail,*
> *Informing his lordship, 'I know what you mane,*
> *Don't fear, noble Brownlow, don't fear them, agra,*
> *For I'll tarnish their laurels,' says Master McGrath.*

As Seamus saw me, he broke off and came over with outstretched arms and a broad smile on his brown wrinkled old face, with its white beard and the curly white hair under his disreputable old hat.

'Jamie, you're a sight for sore eyes! It's good to see you.'

'And you, Seamus,' I said warmly. 'You know, I remember my Granda singing that song to me. Master McGrath was an Irish greyhound, wasn't he?'

'Indeed he was, boy. The greatest of them all, although when he was born his trainer thought nothing of him, he was so small and weakly. But then he confounded them all by winning his races, and his owner, Lord Lurgan, took him over to the most important race, the Waterloo Cup, in 1868. The English owners laughed at him, but

McGrath showed them what he could do by winning the Cup not only that year but two other years, the only dog ever to do as much.'

'You don't hear much about greyhound racing these days, Seamus.'

'That's a fact, boy, but it used to be very popular when I was a lad. Many's the race I've watched, although I never bet on them. They say horse sense is what keeps horses from betting on men, and the same applies to greyhounds. Mind you, I had a friend who nearly ruined himself betting, for all I could say to him.'

'Is this one of your stories, Seamus?'

'Well, it could be. Let's sit down on the river bank over there, and I'll tell it to you, if you like.'

So we strolled on until we reached the river, and there we stretched ourselves out on the bank, looking with delight at the rushing water, and Seamus began his story:

'My friend Barney McCready was a great one for the dogs. Every race he was there – but he could never do anything but lose. He had enough sense not to bet too heavily, so he never ruined himself, but he left himself very hard up. It was no way to live, hardly able to afford butter instead of margarine, or even the odd pint. I had a word with him about it more than once, but although he would agree with me and tell me he was going to stop, it somehow never happened.

Then one day, disaster struck – although it didn't seem like that at first. Barney came rushing into my cottage, beaming all over his face. 'Seamus!' he exclaimed enthusiastically. 'You'll never guess! Sammy Brennan has a new dog, and you wouldn't believe how fast he is. He's one of a litter by *Fast and Furious* out of *Kathleen Flynn* – both winners in their day. He's at least the equal of Master McGrath!

Sammy put on a demonstration for me and I was knocked right back at the speed of him. He's called *Flying Flynn*, and you'd better believe he flies. And what's more, Sammy needs someone to share the price, and he's offered me the chance to buy in. I'll own half of *Flying Flynn*, and I'll get half of the prize money when he wins. I'll be making my fortune!'

'Wait a minute, wait a minute, Barney,' I protested. 'How much does Sammy expect you to pay for a half share in this greyhound?'

'Two thousand punts.'

Now, maybe that doesn't sound too much by today's standards, but at that time it was a whole lot of money.

'And where will you be getting two thousand punts from, Barney?' I asked him, trying to keep my voice calm, although I could hear it getting shrill with horror.

'I'm taking out a mortgage on my cottage, Seamus. I've spoken to Willie Cassidy, and he's ready to lend me the money against the cottage. I'll pay it back monthly out of my winnings on Flynn.' Willie Cassidy was our local bank manager, a sharp, shrewd kind of a man. I knew he wouldn't lend money unless he was sure of getting it back. But in this case, I also knew he wasn't expecting to be paid from *Flying Flynn*'s prize money. He would more likely be expecting to repossess the cottage when Barney wasn't able to pay.

'Barney, have a titter of wit,' I said to him. 'Cancel the arrangements with both Willie and Sammy, or you'll find yourself with no home to live in. When your parents left you the family home, they intended that you'd always have somewhere to live.'

'Seamus, it's not like you to be so pessimistic. I always thought you were a 'glass half full' sort of fella.'

'Well, and so I am,' I told him, 'but only if there's something in the glass to start with. But you've no reason to believe a word Sammy Brennan says about this dog. He's not a man I would trust as far as I could throw him, myself.'

But I could see Barney wasn't listening to me. 'I tell you what, Seamus,' he said. 'I've signed the mortgage agreement with Willie Cassidy, so I'll not be changing that. And I'm going along to see Sammy tomorrow to give him the money. Why don't you come with me and I'll get Sammy to give you a demonstration of how fast *Flynn* is?'

'Okay, Barney, I'll do that,' I agreed.

So the next day I went with Barney, who was on fire with excitement, to see this wonder dog run. Sammy was quite happy to give us a demonstration, and I had to admit that, although *Flying Flynn* was certainly no Master McGrath, he had a fair turn of speed and might easily win a race or two. It was a relief to me that Barney wasn't being taken in by a loser.

'I suppose you might do worse, Barney, if you insist on getting involved with dog racing,' I told him. Barney was already beaming, and could hardly have looked more delighted. I couldn't help adding, 'But maybe you'd be wise to think it over before handing over your money. If you changed your mind you could always pay the money back to Willie Cassidy and cancel your loan.'

But Barney wouldn't hear of it. Ignoring my advice, he produced the cash he had borrowed from the bank, and handed it over to Sammy there and then, and Sammy gave him a signed receipt stating that in return for the payment he was now the legal owner of a half share in *Flying Flynn*. I made my way home, hoping fervently that this wasn't going to backfire on Barney.

It was two weeks later that Barney burst into my house again. But this time, instead of looking excited and happy, he looked utterly miserable.

'Seamus, you'll never believe what's happened,' he groaned. '*Flynn*'s sick, and the vet says he won't be fit to run for several weeks, if ever. And his first big race coming up in a few days' time.'

I was careful not to say I told you so. 'Never mind, Barney,' I said instead. 'There'll be lots more races, and we'll hope he'll recover completely, and be ready to win.'

The next time I saw him, I was glad to see he looked more cheerful. 'Sammy says *Flynn*'s as well as ever,' he told me. 'He thinks the vet was being too pessimistic. He has *Flynn* still in for the race this Saturday. You should come with me to the track in Millerstown to see him win, Seamus.'

Watching dog racing isn't my favourite way to spend an afternoon, but I wanted to support Barney, so along I went.

There was a big crowd, for this was an important race, with a lot of prize money resting on it. Enough, Barney told me, to let him pay off his bank loan. The dogs were clearly excited as they were held by their trainers, ready to be released at the starting order.

'There's *Flynn!*' Barney told me, pointing enthusiastically to where Sammy was holding a straining greyhound, clearly eager to begin running. If it hadn't been Sammy holding him, I wouldn't have recognised him.

Chapter 10 – Flying Flynn

Then they were off, and to Barney's delight (as mine too, for his sake) *Flying Flynn* put on a rare turn of speed right from the start and was soon well out in front.

Just then I heard a voice I recognised speaking behind us. I looked round. It was Peter O'Carroll, the local vet.

'I see Sammy's got hold of another dog to enter instead of *Flynn*,' he was saying to his companion, a fellow vet whom I also knew. 'I didn't notice the name on my list of runners.' He stood, reading down the list for a greyhound under Sammy's name. But before he had finished scouring the list, a burst of excited yells and cheers distracted him, and he looked up to see *Flying Flynn* living up to his name by flying across the finishing line well ahead of the rest of the dogs.

'Barney,' I muttered to him, 'you'd better get away round to the back and warn your friend Sammy that he'd better get that dog he's just been racing under *Flynn*'s name out of sight, before the vet comes round to see him.'

Barney's jaw dropped. 'What?'

'You heard me. There's trouble looming, for you as well as Sammy, I'm afraid. You'll be held equally responsible for the fraud, since you're part owner.'

'F - f - fraud – ?' stammered Barney.

'Sammy's just raced a ringer under *Flynn*'s name – another dog, see? And Peter O'Carroll's about to kick up a fuss about it. So get moving and warn Sammy to hide the animal, quick!'

I've never seen Barney move so fast. Peter O'Carroll, a big, slow moving man, was still explaining to his friend that the dog they had watched winning the race couldn't have been Flying Flynn, whom he had seen lying sick only a few days ago and who couldn't possibly have recovered in the time.

'Och, Peter, could you not just let it go with a private warning to Sammy not to do it again?' asked the friend, who had won a fairly large sum on the dog, whoever he might be.

'No way, Liam,' said Peter, who hadn't. 'I'm going round now to see this dog, and if it's not *Flynn*, I'll report Sammy straight away.'

I followed Peter at a safe distance. In a way, I fully agreed with him. Sammy shouldn't get away with cheating the public. But on the other hand, Barney, who had known nothing about Sammy's substitution of the other dog for his sick runner, didn't deserve to suffer for it, as he undoubtedly would.

I could only be thankful to find that Sammy had packed up in haste and was halfway back to his own headquarters by the time Peter had made his leisurely way to the rear and the kennels where the dogs were kept between races.

By the time Peter followed him and asked to inspect '*Flying Flynn*', Sammy had hidden his new dog – one of the same litter as *Flynn*, and like enough to him in appearance as well as speed – in the furthest kennel, and was all ready to show Peter the real *Flynn* peacefully sleeping.

'The race took it out of him,' Sammy explained glibly. 'It's as well for him to have a thorough rest, and then a good feed when he wakes up in his own time. Especially since he was sick recently – although not so sick as you thought, Peter.'

Peter could say nothing.

But I found plenty to say to Sammy when Peter O'Carroll was safely out of the way. I left him with his promise never to do such a thing again, on penalty of being reported to the authorities – not by the vet, but by me. And I was happy to see that he knew I meant it!

And since *Flynn* recovered completely and went on to win many more races, Barney was happy, too.

11 – Lizzie's Lost Photo

I had driven up to spend a few days in the little Donegal village of Ardnakil, at the small whitewashed cottage I had inherited from my grandparents. The weather had turned cold, after a long warm summer and autumn, but I looked forward to the break from my busy city job. I especially looked forward to meeting up with old friends, in particular my friend Seamus O'Hare.

I've known Seamus since my childhood visits to my grandparents, and what knowledge I had of the countryside, its flowers and wildlife, came from him. He was a poacher, but a man with a heart of gold.

When I had settled into the cottage, I took a stroll along the country lanes, their hedges bright with red hawthorn berries, until I came to Ardnakil village, where the river runs through the main street, and the warm, welcoming sight of *The Golden Pheasant* inn. Pushing open the door, I went in, and was rewarded by Seamus's voice from the corner, 'Jamie, boy! Come away in. You're a sight for sore eyes.'

I got myself a pint of the black stuff from the bar, and sat down beside him. 'It's great to see you, Seamus,' I said. We exchanged our news, and then I said, 'Seamus, can you remind me of the barman's name? I should certainly know it after the years I've been coming here, but my mind's a complete blank.'

'Barney Mulligan,' Seamus told me.

'Of course! Seamus, whether it's because I've been working too hard or what, I find I'm forgetting more and more things recently. Not just names. I put an important file away last week, and when I needed it I couldn't for the life of me think where it was. Well, it turned up, but more by accident than anything else. Do you think it's old age coming on?' I was laughing as I spoke, for I'm still a young man.

'Och, it's the sort of thing that happens to all of us, boy. A bit of a break and you'll be fine,' Seamus assured me. 'But it's true forgetfulness grows on us all as we get older. My friend Lizzie Brennan, for instance, although she isn't more than twenty years older than me, started to get very forgetful some time ago. And at least once her forget-fulness made her very unhappy.'

'Is there a story, Seamus?'

'There is. I'll tell it to you if you like.' He took another sip, and began:

'Lizzie lived by herself in a cottage not far from mine, and when I was a youngster trying to get by after both my parents died, she was kindness itself to me. She would bring me in for the odd meal, and gave me warm clothes that had been her brother Pat's. Pat had gone to America to make his fortune not long after their parents died.

Lizzie was lonely, as even I could tell, and one cold day when we were sitting by her turf fire, she told me the real reason why.

It seemed that Lizzie had been engaged to be married to one of her brother's friends, Declan Harvey, but Declan, like so many in those days, couldn't get a job at home and felt that he couldn't afford to get married until he made some money. When Pat began to talk about going to America, Declan thought he should follow Pat's example and go, too.

Lizzie tried to persuade him to stay and try to make a living at home, but he had his mind set on going and nothing she could say would persuade him. So off he went, and the years passed, and even-tually Lizzie became convinced she would never see him again. It was about that time Brian Doyle appeared on the scene. He'd bought one of the local farms and settled in Ardnakil, and straight away he showed that he was very keen on Lizzie.

'Och, Brian,' she said when he first proposed, 'do you not see the ring on my finger? I'm engaged, man dear.'

'And how long is it since you've heard from the same man?' Brian Doyle asked her, and Lizzie admitted it was a long time.

'But he's not much of a letter writer, Brian,' she said. 'I get messages from him in Pat's letters, sometimes.'

'And when was the last time he sent a message?' Brian persisted, and Lizzie realised how long it was.

That night she took out her most precious possession, a snapshot of Declan he'd given her just before he left, and looked at it earnestly.

The next day I was round at her cottage, and she shared her problem with me. 'What should I do, Seamus? Do you think Declan's just forgotten me?'

'I'm sure he hasn't done that, Lizzie,' I said. I was no longer a child by then, but I was still young enough to be romantic. 'He'd not just let you down when he was so in love with you. But maybe he's been ill or something. Why don't you write and ask Pat if he knows what's happening?'

'I'll do that, Seamus,' Lizzie said, and that very night she wrote off to her brother Pat.

Pat took his time about answering, but at last a letter came. I happened to call round just after Lizzie had got it, and found her in tears.

'Och, Seamus, it's awful bad news. Pat says Declan went off on his own a few years ago, to try his fortune in the West. Pat has a decent job in Boston, I told you, didn't I? In the police force. Declan didn't fancy that, so off he went and Pat hasn't heard of him from that day to this. He says he's afraid Declan may have got into trouble or maybe even been killed in an accident.'

I did my best to comfort her, but there was little I could say. 'Pat's only guessing, Lizzie,' was the best I could do, but she paid no attention.

'He'd have kept in touch with Pat if he still cared about me,' she said. 'Well,' she wiped away her tears and made a brave effort to smile, 'it's good I still have a man like Brian Doyle to fall back on.'

And the next time Brian Doyle called round, Lizzie told him that she'd been thinking it over, and she'd marry him if he still wanted her to.

Brian was delighted, and before long it was all fixed up, and Lizzie became Lizzie Doyle. She seemed happy enough, but I couldn't help feeling that there was a certain sadness lurking behind her smiles.

Well, time went on, and Brian and Lizzie were as happy as most, although Lizzie confided to me that she would have liked some children. But somehow it wasn't to be.

To tell you the truth, I'd forgotten all about Lizzie's first romance, and when in the course of time Brian Doyle died and left her the farm, Lizzie took it very well. She told me, for we'd kept in touch and she still shared her feelings with me, that she missed Brian, but more and more her thoughts kept going back to Declan.

When she decided to marry Brian, she'd put the snapshot Declan had given her away somewhere out of sight and out of mind, for she didn't believe, as a married woman, she should be thinking about another man.

'Yes, you did right there, Lizzie,' I nodded.

'But now all that's over – and I was happy with Brian, and I miss him, Seamus – still, I don't think there'd be any harm now in me getting out the photo and remembering happy times, long gone.'

'No harm at all, Lizzie,' I assured her. 'I wouldn't mind having a look myself, for it's so long ago I hardly remember what Declan Harvey looked like.'

'I'll hunt it out now,' Lizzie said suddenly. She didn't spring up, for she'd aged a lot and was far from being the active lass she'd been when I first knew her, but, there, I wasn't a youngster any more, myself, by then.

'It won't be with the rest of my photos, for I put it away somewhere different so it wouldn't keep turning up,' she said, as she began to hunt through drawers and on shelves.

After a while, I could see she was getting upset, so I stood up to help her, but even with both of us hunting everywhere we could think of, there was neither hide nor hair of that photograph.

'I'm getting so forgetful these days,' Lizzie said. 'I can hardly remember the names of my best friends, sometimes. Old age, I suppose. Happens to us all. But where can I have put the photo? You don't think I'd have thrown it out by mistake, Seamus?'

'No, why would you do that, Lizzie? I tell you what, give it a rest just now, and tomorrow when you're feeling fresher you can have another look.'

So Lizzie agreed, and we sat down again to a welcome cup of tea before I took my leave of her.

But although she hunted the house top to bottom, the photo didn't turn up, and at last Lizzie had to give up.

It was some months later that I strolled into *The Golden Pheasant* and saw a tall, elderly man sitting at the bar who looked vaguely familiar. It was no one local, and for a while I couldn't put a name to him. He was talking to Barney, and it seemed he'd been asking Barney for information. As I listened I noticed that his accent was an odd mixture of Irish and American.

'The trouble is, Barney, that I know she married, but I never heard her husband's name. And of course she's moved away from the cottage she lived in when I knew her.'

'Well, I wish I could help you, boyo,' Barney said, 'but a Christian name on its own isn't much to go on. There are a good many Lizzies around Ardnakil.'

Lizzie! The stranger was looking for someone called Lizzie! I took another good look at him, and light burst on me. I went over to him.

'It's Declan Harvey, isn't it?' I said. 'You'll maybe not remember me, for I was just a wee skitter when you left for America – Seamus O'Hare, if that rings any bells.'

'Seamus! I wouldn't have known you! But now I take a good look at you, I can see the resemblance. Seamus, you'll have a pint with me.'

We sat down together with our pints, and the more I looked at him the more I recognised him. He'd picked up a bit of an American accent, as folks do, but the local voice was still there beneath it.

'So, Declan, did I hear that you're looking to meet up again with someone called Lizzie?'

'Well, yes, I am, Seamus. You remember that I was engaged to young Lizzie Brennan before I went off to America. It's a long story, but I broke my leg badly out in the wilds of the western states, and was in hospital for the best part of a year before they had me fixed up again. And it took me a while to make contact with Lizzie's brother Pat, for he'd changed his address by then. And when I did finally track him down through a friend we both knew, he told me Lizzie was married. It broke my heart, Seamus, but I suppose I was glad for her that she'd found a good man.'

'But why did you not write to Lizzie herself, Declan, instead of relying on Pat to keep you in touch?'

'Och, Seamus, I was young and stupid. I'd gone off to make a fortune for Lizzie, and I was ashamed to admit that far from that, I was worse off than ever, for I owed the hospital a huge amount for fixing my leg.' He paused and sighed. 'I've done all right since then, in fact I'm well off now, but I thought I'd like to see Lizzie again, just for old times' sake. The last thing I want is to butt in on her marriage, but I thought I could apologise and ask her to forgive me, and maybe be friends.'

Well, I thought I'd better put him out of his misery straightaway. 'Lizzie's been a widow these two years, Declan,' I said. 'And I know there's nothing she'd like better than to meet you again. She hasn't forgotten you, whatever else she may forget.'

I've never seen such a beam of happiness on a face before. But it was nothing to the joy that lit up Lizzie's face when she saw him and heard his story.

Needless to say, they were married shortly afterwards. As for the snapshot, it turned up later when Lizzie was spring cleaning – it had slipped down the back of a drawer. But pleased as Lizzie was to get it, it didn't really matter as much as it had. After all, she had the real thing now.

12 – A play for Christmas

Christmas was coming closer every day as I sat with my friend Seamus O'Hare at the glowing turf fire he had lit in the hearth of his tumble-down cottage. The warmth of it crept over my legs and I leaned back with a sigh of satisfaction in the soft old armchair and wrapped my hands round my mug of hot tea.

'There's nowhere like Ardnakil at Christmas time, Seamus,' I said happily.

I'd been coming up to the little Donegal village of Ardnakil, to the small whitewashed cottage left to me by my grandparents, since the far off days when I used to visit them as a child, and I'd known Seamus since then, when he used to tell me about the birds and flowers of the countryside. As well as that, he'd spun me many a tale about the doings of himself and his friends, for Seamus was a *Seanachie*, which is the Irish for storyteller.

'It's just a pity you have to rush off before the day, boy,' Seamus answered me, 'but I know you want to spend Christmas with your family.'

'Yes, I know I'm missing some things, Seamus.'

'Especially the Christmas play, this year, boy.'

'Oh, I didn't know you had a play at Christmas, Seamus.'

'It's not every year that we have. Indeed, this will be the first for many's a year. It just depends if we have a few people keen to do a bit of acting. Some of the youngsters have got together and formed an amateur company, *The Ardnakil Players,* just recently. There used to be a company of the same name when I was a much younger man, and they put on some fine plays.

The best of the lot, I'd say, was one got up by a young girl of the name of Hazel Kilpatrick. Hazel was full of energy. She not only wrote this play herself, but she got a group together to act it, and she played the leading role. Mind you, the whole thing nearly came to grief.'

'This sounds like a story, Seamus. Tell me more.'

Seamus settled back comfortably into his chair on the other side of the hearth, took a pull at his disreputable old pipe, and ran his hand through his curly white hair, his bright eyes twinkling. 'Sure, Jamie, you expect me to pull another story out of the hat every time I see you.'

'And you never disappoint me, Seamus. So on you go!'

'Well, then, Hazel had loved acting since she was a little girl at the village school, where the teacher would sometimes get the children to perform plays as part of their lessons, and everyone said how good she was. It was the desire of her heart to be what she called 'a real actress', and go on the professional stage. She must have been eighteen, I suppose, when she decided that an amateur company would be good practice for her, and she got *The Ardnakil Players* together.

I was more than twice her age, and she looked on me as a father, her own having died when she was young. She used to come round sometimes and sit where you are now, boy, and tell me her hopes and dreams. She would have loved to go to Dublin and try her fortune there when she left school, but her mother, Aggie Kilpatrick, wouldn't hear of it, and Hazel had to go into a dress shop in Millerstown when she was fifteen. In spite of this, Hazel was a cheerful, chirpy sort of girl, with long flowing red hair which she tied back in the shop, but which at other times she let loose around her shoulders.

I well remember when she first showed me the play she'd been writing, about a girl who had been stolen from her wealthy parents and brought up in poverty, until at last they found her. It was a sort of Cinderella story, and you probably think it doesn't sound up to much, but nearly every other line had a joke in it, and most of the rest would have broken your heart, so that when Hazel read me out some of the bits, I was between laughing and crying, listening to her beautiful voice.

'It'll take some organising, I know,' Hazel said. 'I can easily get people to act the parts – I've already cast them all in my own mind, and I know they'll be good, especially Johnny Clarke in the hero's role. It's the back stage people who'll be hard to rope in. I'll need someone to help with the costumes, and someone to do the scenery, and someone for the props. And then we'll need someone for the box office and someone else to take the tickets at the door and show people to their seats. I've got people in mind for most of that, but I just hope I can get them to agree to do it.'

'Och, you'll have no problem, Hazel. Who could say no to a cheeky youngster like yourself?' I said, and indeed although I made a joke of it, it was true enough that Hazel had a way with her, and could talk anyone into what she wanted, as a general rule.

Everything seemed to be going well, until just a few days before the show was due to go on, and then things suddenly went wrong. Hazel came round to see me with the tears tripping her.

'You know my Ma's best friend Shelagh MacCartney, Seamus? She was going to take the tickets on the way in and show people to their seats, while Ma ran the box office. But sure, didn't they have the father and mother of a row last night, and now neither of them is speaking to the other, and Ma says she won't have anything more to do with the play if Shelagh MacCartney's part of the setup. And Shelagh says she'd be very happy to pull out, so don't expect to see her again. I don't know what to do. There's nobody left to ask. All my friends are already helping.'

That was true enough. I'd have offered to run the box office myself, or take the tickets, but I was already lined up to set up the scenery and shift it between scenes, and even I couldn't be in two places at once.

'Och, Seamus, what am I going to do?' Hazel wailed.

'Maybe it'll all blow over,' I said. 'Was it anything serious?'

'Not in the least!' Hazel said. 'That Biddy O'Neill told Ma that Shelagh had said Ma's new hairstyle made her look like something dragged through the hedge backwards, and at first Shelagh said she'd said nothing of the sort, and then she went into a huff and refused to apologise or anything, and now Ma's flaming! And the rest of them, the actors and everybody, are starting to take sides too, and next thing some of them will be refusing to take part. It looks as if I'm going to have to call the whole thing off!'

'Don't be doing that, now, Hazel. Maybe if I had a word with the two ladies?' I offered. 'Sure, this is no time of year to be holding grudges instead of forgiving each other.'

'Could you, Seamus?' asked Hazel tearfully. 'It might help – I don't know.'

I patted her hand. 'Don't worry about it any more, love,' I said. 'It's Christmas – we should expect to be seeing some of that peace on earth the angels sang about.' And Hazel went home comforted a bit.

Thinking it over, it seemed to me the person at the root of the whole thing was Shelagh MacCartney, so it was Shelagh I went round to see first, the next day.

I had reasons of my own for wanting Hazel's play to be successful. I'd invited an old friend of mine to come and see it, and I didn't want him to be disappointed.

I caught up with Shelagh doing her shopping in the village, and invited her into the café for a cup of tea, an invitation which she seemed delighted to accept.

'I hear Biddy O'Neill's been spreading lies about you, Shelagh,' I began cautiously. 'Mind you, Biddy probably got the whole thing wrong. She's a bit deaf, you know. She seems to think you said something bad about Aggie Kilpatrick's hair.'

Shelagh looked ready to burst into tears. 'Och, Seamus, I never said anything bad about Aggie's hair!' she wailed. 'All I said was that Aggie had a new hairdo, that would charm the birds out of the hedges!'

'Hush, now, Shelagh, people are looking at us,' I warned her. 'Well, Shelagh, why don't you tell Aggie that?'

Shelagh shook her head firmly. 'If Aggie can believe I said bad things about her, when we've been friends for over forty years since we first started school, then I'm not going to start explaining myself to her. It's for her to say sorry to me for believing that Biddy O'Neill.'

I gave up on Shelagh for the time being. At least I'd heard the truth as to what Shelagh actually said. So I went to call on Biddy O'Neill.

Biddy was out feeding her hens when I got there.

'Let me carry that bucket for you, Biddy,' I said, taking the bucket of feed from her. 'My, but your hens are looking right and perky.'

Biddy looked pleased. 'You're a gentleman, Seamus,' she said.

'But I hear people have been spreading some gossip about you, old friend,' I went on. 'I knew it couldn't be right as soon as I heard it, so I thought I'd better warn you.'

'What do you mean, Seamus?'

'Why, that you told Aggie Kilpatrick that Shelagh MacCartney said her hair looked like something pulled through a hedge backwards. But Shelagh tells me what she said was that Aggie's new hairstyle could charm the birds from the hedges.'

Biddy looked surprised. 'Was that what she said? I knew it was something about hedges.'

'Well, Biddy, d'ye think maybe you heard it a bit wrong?'

'That could be, Seamus, for, mind you, I've been getting sort of deaf lately, though I wouldn't say so to anyone but you, who won't spread it round. I'd be that embarrassed if people knew.'

'So, Biddy, maybe you could tell Aggie you could have been mistaken in what you told her?'

'Och, Seamus, I wouldn't like to do that. Aggie might start telling people I'm deaf and really I'm just a wee bit hard of hearing. I can make people out if they speak up properly, like you, Seamus.'

'Have you thought to getting the doctor to look at your ears, Biddy? Maybe the problem's only wax.'

'Seamus, that's a great idea.'

'Well, supposing I explained to Aggie, and got her to promise not to mention about your hearing to anyone?'

'Sure, that would be fine, Seamus – as long as she promises.'

So round I took myself to my last port of call, Aggie herself. I found her indoors, having a cup of tea.

'Come away in, Seamus, and have a cup with me,' she greeted me. I wasted no time, but explained clearly to her that because of Biddy O'Neill's deafness, which she didn't want known, Shelagh's words had been completely twisted.

'It's like that game we sometimes play at Christmas parties, Chinese Whispers. If you pass on something you haven't heard properly, it comes out all wrong. Shelagh was paying you a lovely compliment, Aggie, and it's natural she should be hurt that you'd believe otherwise.'

'Well, I suppose that makes a difference,' Aggie said slowly. 'I'd like to believe well of Shelagh. But as for that Biddy O'Neill – !'

'Now, now, Aggie, don't be starting a quarrel with Biddy instead of Shelagh, especially at Christmas time! Biddy should have more sense than to repeat something she hasn't heard properly, but sure she meant no harm. People will have to learn to take anything she says with a grain of salt. And Biddy's helping with the costumes for Hazel's play, so we don't want her walking out either.'

Aggie's face showed that she'd got my point.

'Hazel's play matters to her,' I said. 'You're her mother, Aggie. You don't want to spoil it for her.'

'No, I don't, Seamus,' Aggie said. 'I'll go round and sort things out with Shelagh now. And neither of us will quarrel with Biddy, much as she deserves it.'

So everything was fine and on the night the play went wonderfully well. And one of the most enthusiastic of the audience was my friend Matt Kennedy, the well known actor, who'd come down from Dublin for it on my invitation. I took him round to meet Hazel after the performance, and straightaway he offered her a part in his next production.

Hazel was over the moon, and when Aggie saw the happiness in her face, she couldn't stand in her way any more. So there was peace all round, after all, that Christmas – especially after Biddy got her ears syringed!

About the author

Gerry McCullough has been writing poems and stories since childhood. Brought up in north Belfast, she graduated in English and Philosophy from Queen's University, Belfast, then went on to gain an MA in English.

She lives in Northern Ireland – in a converted stone-built cottage in the heart of Co. Down – has four grown up children and is married to author, media producer and broadcaster, Raymond McCullough, with whom she co-edited the Irish magazine, *Bread*, from 1990-96. In 1995 they also published a non-fiction book called, *Ireland – now the good news!*

Over the past few years Gerry has had more than one hundred and forty short stories published in UK, Irish and American magazines, anthologies and annuals – as well as broadcast on *BBC Radio Ulster* – plus poems and articles published in several Northern Ireland and UK magazines. She has also read from her novels, poems and short stories at many Irish literary events.

Gerry won the *Cúirt International Literary Award* for 2005 (Galway); was shortlisted for the 2008 *Brian Moore Award* (Belfast); shortlisted for the 2009 *Cúirt Award*; commended in the 2009 *Seán O'Faolain Short Story Competition*, (Cork) and shortlisted in the 2015 *Harmony House Poetry Competition*, Downpatrick. In 2016 she also won the *Bangor Poetry Award* for her poem, *Summer Passing*.

Gerry currently has a total of twenty books in publication –

Stand alone romantic suspense novels (4):

- *Belfast Girls* (November 2010, re-issued July 2012)
- *Danger Danger* (October 2011)
- *Johnny McClintock's War* (August 2014)
- *Roundabout* (July 2020)

The Angel Murphy thriller series (3):

- *Angel in Flight* (June 2012)
- *Angel in Belfast* (June 2013)
- *Angel in Paradise* (January 2017)
- *Angel on Guard* (October 2023)

The Hel's Heroes romantic comedy series (2):

- *Hel's Heroes: a romantic comedy* (June 2015)
- *Hel's Heroes 2: Christie and the Pirate* (March 2019)

Short story collections (7):

- *The Seanachie: Tales of Old Seamus* (January 2012)
- *The Seanachie 2: Norah on the Beach & other stories* (September 2014)
- *The Seanachie 3: Seamus and the Shell & other stories* (August 2016)
- *The Seanachie 4: Paddy and the Snake & other stories* (June 2019)
- *The Seanachie 5: Seamus Makes a Mistake & other stories* (November 2021)
- *The Seanachie 6: In the Bluebell Wood & other stories* (September 2023)
- *A Seanachie Christmas: A seasonal collection of 'Tales of Old Seamus'* (December 2023)
- *Dreams, Visions, Nightmares* – a collection of eight literary and award-winning Irish short stories (January 2016)

Fantasy novels (2):

- *Not the End of the World* – a comic, futuristic fantasy novel (February 2016)
- *Lady Molly and the Snapper* – a young adult novel, time travel adventure set in Dublin and the open sea (August 2012)

Roundabout:
a modern day Vanity Fair

Like *Vanity Fair*, there is no hero or heroine – a story of love, comedy, drama – in fact, life! Some characters you will find sympathetic, some you may detest!

Millie and Sooze, set out on their separate ventures into life – meeting Josh, Danny, Johnny, Tommy and several others.

For some of these people, their ride on the roundabout of life ends well – for others it doesn't.

Is there more to life's roundabout than pleasure or misery?

"well written, characters seem real ... unique in bringing the story bang up to date. Any fan of the original will delight in the new telling of a classic tale."
Trevor Belshaw, *Amazon, UK*

"shows a depth of empathy with these people she's created, this brings the book alive"
S. Burke, *Goodreads Author, Australia*

"a clever updating of a classic tale. Highly recommended as escape reading"
Barbara Silkstone, *Amazon.com*

"Engaging, contemporary style of writing that works splendidly in this modern take on Vanity Fair "
Margaret Sharp, *Goodreads Author, Australia*

Read the first chapter of **Roundabout**:

Roundabout

a modern day Vanity Fair

Gerry McCullough

Published by

Precious Oil

PUBLICATIONS

www.preciousoil.com/publications

Roundabout
A modern day *Vanity Fair* – set in Ireland

Like *Vanity Fair*, there is no hero or heroine – a story of love, comedy, drama – in fact, life! Some characters you will find sympathetic, some you may detest!

Millie and Sooze, set out on their separate ventures into life – meeting Josh, Danny, Johnny, Tommy and several others.

For some of these people, their ride on the roundabout of life ends well – for others it doesn't.

Is there more to life's roundabout than pleasure or misery?

"well written, characters seem real ... unique in bringing the story bang up to date. Any fan of the original will delight in the new telling of a classic tale."
Trevor Belshaw, *Amazon, UK*

"shows a depth of empathy with these people she's created, this brings the book alive"
S. Burke, *Goodreads Author, Australia*

"a clever updating of a classic tale. Highly recommended as escape reading"
Barbara Silkstone, *Amazon.com*

"Engaging, contemporary style of writing that works splendidly in this modern take on Vanity Fair "
Margaret Sharp, *Goodreads Author, Australia*

Come and watch the Roundabout. The people are beginning to climb on board. They sit on horseback, on lions, in motorcars.

Listen! – the music is starting. The roundabout begins – round and round, back to the start, then round again. The people are clinging on tightly, afraid to let go – except for those who know what's coming next for them.

Most of them start off expecting good things – expecting to enjoy themselves. But after a round or two, they realise something is missing. They are no longer sure if the ride alone is something to enjoy or not.

Chapter One

Millicent Brennan and Susan O'Leary left *St Bernadette's Convent School for Girls* in Belfast on the same day. It was the end of June. The sun was bright, the beds were full of fragrant smelling flowers, sweet peas, tulips, pansies, marigolds. They had both turned eighteen in the last year and had now completed their A Level exams. The results would not be out for a couple of months yet.

Millie was a tall, slim, red haired girl with green eyes which had a wicked gleam. She was dressed in the Saint Bernadette's school uniform, not by choice but for lack of anything else. Her uniform didn't fit her very well. It was too big, and the skirt draggled round her slim, excellent legs.

Sooze was shorter, stockier, but nevertheless attractive, dark haired and blue eyed, with a sweet face hard to resist. She was also wearing school uniform, but in her case it was because she felt it was appropriate to wear it until she had actually left. In any case, hers, made to measure by an excellent dressmaker, fitted perfectly.

They had not previously been close friends, but recently Millie had made an effort to develop some sort of friendship with Sooze.

'Sooze, I do love the way you're doing your hair recently. It really suits you.'

'Oh, Millie, do you really think so?'

'Of course! I never say things I don't mean. You should know that by now, Sooze!'

After a week or two of that sort of thing she said, looking sad but brave, 'Oh, Sooze, I wish I knew where I was going to stay when they chuck us out of school. After boarding for years here – and now that my Dad's passed on

– I really have nowhere to go. Och, well,' – with a tearful smile – 'I'm sure I'll find somewhere!'

Sooze had a tender heart. She felt a pang for Millie at once, and burst out without thinking, 'Why don't you come to stay with us for a while until you get yourself sorted, Millie? We have tons of room.'

'Oh, Sooze, do you really mean it? But would your parents want me? You'd have to ask them first, wouldn't you?'

'Well, I suppose I'd better. But I'm sure they'd be happy to have you.' Having Millie in the house wouldn't be a problem for Sooze, who wouldn't even think of doing any of the extra work. What else were the staff for? And she didn't expect her parents to object. All her life she'd been used to them giving her everything she'd ever wanted.

Millie pressed her friend's hand gratefully. She knew a little about Sooze's parents. Enough to think that an invitation to stay with them might open a few doors for her. John O'Leary was a high flying businessman, well off and powerful. His wife was in a position to buy the latest fashions and to appear regularly in photographs in the *Ulster Tatler*. They had a lifestyle which Sooze took for granted, but which Millie envied with all her heart.

Millie's parents were a very different story. Her father, Charlie Brennan – an unsuccessful rock musician who had been killed when he crashed his motorbike a year ago – had taught music to the girls of St Bernadette's two days a week, and had made himself so popular with the nuns – in particular the Mother Superior, headmistress of the school – that he had managed to persuade her to take in his little Millie as a pupil without charge, and to continue to keep her even after his own death. Charlie had been a man of great charm, but since he had never been able to keep a pound in his pocket for more than a few hours or so, he had left Millie equally penniless.

She had been glad enough to have her education continued in a school which ranked as one of the best girls' schools in Northern Ireland. As for Millie's mother, who had died when Millie was still a child, the less said about her the better, according to the Reverend Mother. She had been a singer who had met Charlie Brennan on tour, and had lived with him until the drug habit she had been unable to shake off finished her. Millie had inherited her singing voice but not, she was glad to say, her addictions.

Before girls left St Bernadette's, it was the custom for the head-mistress to call each leaver into her study, and give them a little lecture on what was expected from every St Bernadette's girl going out into the world, and how she should conduct herself to bring honour to the school. Then Mother Veronica would solemnly present each one with a copy of a DVD she had had specially made, with a sermon from Father Connelly, who supervised the religious teaching of the school, together with a speech she herself had delivered at the preceding prize giving day.

'If you listen to this regularly, my dear,' she said to each girl, 'it will keep you on the right track.'

Sooze received her DVD with appropriate awe. Her habit had been to respect the Reverend Mother and to swallow everything she said.

'Oh, thank you, Mother Veronica!' she said earnestly. 'I'll treasure this.'

And Mother Veronica beamed benignly.

As Sooze left the study, the headmistress turned majestically to her assistant, the meek, rabbit like Sister Angelica.

'And I think that was the last of this year's school leavers, sister,' she said.

'Oh, but, Mother Superior …' Sister Angelica murmured in a small frightened voice, 'what about Millicent Brennan?'

'Millicent Brennan?' The headmistress's frown was awe inspiring. 'Millicent Brennan does not deserve a copy of my DVD. It would be impossible to give that girl anything which would prevent her from going from bad to worse. Mark my words, sister, whenever we hear anything about that girl in the future, it will be all bad. I kept her here for her father's sake, but I'll be only too glad to see the back of her.'

Millie had committed the unforgivable crime of being rude to the Reverend Mother, and had even been caught imitating her to a group of girls, behind Mother Veronica's back.

Sister Angelica was near to tears. Much as she had had to suffer from Millie's cheekiness herself, she couldn't bear to see the girl sent off into the world without the support of the precious DVD. Dear Charlie Brennan's daughter, too! Charlie had been such a sweet man.

So when the Reverend Mother had departed to carry out some further duty, Sister Angelica slipped back into the study, opened the cup-board where the DVD's were kept, and removed one from the top of the enormous pile. One would not be missed.

She hurried out to the entrance hall, and was glad to see Millie and Sooze, their luggage piled around them, still waiting for John O'Leary's limousine to collect them.

'Millicent, dear! The Reverend Mother has had to hurry off to see to something – an emergency which has come up suddenly. So she asked me to see that you got a copy of her DVD. We couldn't allow you to leave without one. Susan already has hers, don't you dear?'

Sister Angelica soothed her conscience for the white lie by telling herself that she couldn't allow the poor child to be so hurt.

Millie took the DVD from Sister Angelica's outstretched hand. Her expression was hard to read.

'Please listen to it regularly, Millicent,' Sister Angelica said earnestly. 'As the Reverend Mother always says, it will help to keep you on the right path.'

A uniformed chauffeur came in through the main door as she finished speaking.

Sooze hurried over to him, followed by Millie.

'Hello, Kelly!' she greeted him smilingly. 'You're in great time. This is my friend Millie who's coming to stay with me for a while.'

'Hello, Millie,' said Tommy Kelly. The chauffeur was a tall, good looking man with dark hair and a sexy smile. Millie liked the look of him. She gave him her best smile in return, and to her pleasure he returned it with a wink. 'Now, let's get these suitcases out to the car.'

By the time they had everything loaded, Mother Veronica had come out onto the steps which led to the huge, impressive entrance door of St Bernadette's, ready to wave graciously to her best – i.e. most wealthy – pupil (although not, she was disappointed to see, to either of her distinguished parents).

She waved regally, noticing with disapproval that Millicent Brennan had apparently managed to wriggle her way into Susan O'Leary's car and must be getting a lift with her. She stood for a moment while the car began to move. A window rolled down and a hand was thrust out of it. The hand was holding a small object.

A second later, the object came whizzing through the air to strike Mother Veronica on her chest. Mother Veronica gasped with horror as the thing slid down her front and smashed onto the top step. She took an involuntary step backwards and looked down at the ruined object.

It was her DVD.

Belfast Girls

Gerry McCullough
author of Angel Series and the Danny Series

The story of three girls – Sheila, Phil and Mary – growing up into the new emerging post-conflict Belfast of money, drugs, high fashion and crime; and of their lives and loves.

Sheila, a supermodel, is kidnapped. Phil is sent to prison. Mary, surviving a drug overdose, has a spiritual awakening.

It is also the story of the men who matter to them –

John Branagh, former candidate for the priesthood, a modern Darcy, someone to love or hate. Will he and Sheila ever get together? Davy Hagan, drug dealer, 'mad, bad and dangerous to know'. Is Phil also mad to have anything to do with him?

Although from different religious backgrounds, starting off as childhood friends, the girls manage to hold on to that friendship in spite of everything.

A book about contemporary Ireland and modern life. A book which both men and women can enjoy - thriller, romance, comedy, drama - and much more ….

"fascinating ... original ... multilayered ... expertly travels from one genre to the next"

Kellie Chambers, Ulster Tatler (Book of the Month)

"romance at the core ... enriched with breathtaking action, mystery, suspense and some tear-jerking moments of tragedy.

Sheila M. Belshaw, author

"What starts out as a crime thriller quickly evolves into a literary festival beyond the boundary of genres"

PD Allen, author

https://smarturl.it/BelfastGirls

Danger Danger

Gerry McCullough

Two lives in parallel – twin sisters separated at birth, but their lives take strangely similar and dangerous roads until the final collision which hurls each of them to the edge of disaster.

Katie and her gambling boyfriend Dec find themselves threatened with peril from the people Dec has cheated.

Jo-Anne (Annie) through her boyfriend Steven finds herself in the hands of much more dangerous crooks.

Can they survive and achieve safety and happiness?

"starts with a bang and never quite lets up on the tension ... it will hook you from the beginning and keep you spell bound until the very last sentence."

Ellen Fritz, Books 4 Tomorrow

"The emotional intensity of the characters is beautifully drawn ... You care for these people."
Stacey Danson, *author*

an amazing, page turning, stunning novel ... equal to Belfast Girls *in every respect. I can't wait for her next novel to be published.*

Teresa Geering, *author*

an attention-grabbing plot, strong writing, and vivid characterization, ... fast-paced and highly addictive

L. Anne Carrington, *author*

Johnny McClintock's WAR

One man's struggle against the hammer blows of life

The story of one man's struggle to maintain his faith in spite of everything life throws at him.

As the outbreak of the First World War looms closer, John Henry McClintock, a Northern Irish Protestant by upbringing, meets Rose Flanagan, a Catholic, at a gospel tent mission – and falls in love with her.

When Johnny enlists and sets off to fight in the War he finds himself surrounded by death and tragedy, which pushes his trust in God to the limit.

After more than five years absence he returns home to a bitter, war torn Ireland, where both he and Rose are seen as traitors to their own sides.

John Henry and Rose overcome all opposition and, finally, marry. But a few years later comes the hardest blow of all. Can John Henry still hang on to his faith in God?

"brilliant .. this book had me captured from the start .. moves at a fair pace throughout"
Tom Elder, *Amazon.com*

"characters you will truly care about ..

a gut-wrenching emotional ride .. a must read"

Tom Winton, author, USA

"Gerry McCullough's best book yet ..
a powerful tribute to those who died for their countries and what they believed"
Juliet B Madison, author, UK

"an emotional roller coaster ride .. an epiphany .. highly recommended
.. a book that will make you think about how wonderful life truly is"
Thomas Baker, Amazon.com, Santiago, Chile

"will hold you spellbound until the very last sentence .. I love this book"
Sheila Mary Belshaw, author, UK, Menorca, Cape Town

Angel in Flight:

the first Angel Murphy thriller

Gerry McCullough

Is it a bird? Is it a plane? No, it's a low-flying Angel!

You've heard of Lara Croft. You've heard of Modesty Blaise. Well, here comes Angel Murphy!

Angel, a *'feisty wee Belfast girl'* on holiday in Greece, sorts out a villain who wants to make millions for his pharmaceutical company by preventing the use of a newly discovered malaria vaccine.

Angel has a broken marriage behind her and is wary of men, but perhaps her meeting with Josh Smith, who tells her he's with Interpol, may change her mind?

Fun, action, thrills, romance in a beautiful setting – so much to enjoy!

"it's a fast-paced read, ... exciting, and you can not put this book down"

Thomas Baker, Santiago, Chile

"I could not stop reading! ... a gripping thriller from beginning to the end"
SanMarie Lamprecht

"a fast-paced, exciting read. From the moment I read the first line, I was hooked"

Cheryl Bradshaw, author, Wyoming, USA

"a sassy bigger then life heroine in an action packed adventure thriller in Greece"

Book Review Buzz

Angel in Belfast:

the 2nd Angel Murphy thriller

Gerry McCullough

Angel Murphy is back, in true kick boxing form!

Alone in his cottage near a remote Irish village, Fitz, lead singer of the popular band *Raving*, hears the cries of the paparazzi outside and likens them in his own mind to wolves in a feeding frenzy.

Next morning Fitz is found unconscious, seeming unlikely to survive, and is rushed to hospital. Has he been driven to OD? Or is someone else behind this?

His friends call in Angeline Murphy, 'Angel to her friends, devil to her enemies,' to find out the truth. But it takes all Angel's courage and skills to survive the many dangers she faces and to discover the real villain and deal with him.

"brings the city and its people ... to life with evocative description and scintillating dialogue"

Elinor Carlisle, Berkshire,UK

"I could not stop reading! ... a gripping thriller from beginning to the end"

SanMarie Lamprecht

"makes the troubled city of Belfast vibrant and appealing"

P A Lanstone, UK

"I felt like I had been transported to Belfast's often tough, gritty streets"

Bobbi Lerman, USA

"love the fact that we are reintroduced to characters from Belfast Girls"

Michele Young, UK

"so well written that you find yourself flying through the stories"

Tom Elder

Angel in Paradise:

the 3rd Angel Murphy thriller

Angeline Murphy, 'Angel to her friends, devil to her enemies,' is on holiday in Corfu with her friend Josh Smith, hoping to relax and recharge her batteries, and perhaps develop her relationship with Josh.

But Angel finds it impossible to sit back and do nothing when she learns of the assault and robbery carried out on her parents' old friend Sophie.

Before long Angel is fully involved in tracking down the brutal gang of jewel thieves who are terrorising many of the island's elderly but wealthy inhabitants. Her plan is, with Josh's help, to identify and arrest the gang's leader.

But soon Angel is in serious danger herself, from men who don't hesitate to kill to cover their tracks.

And meanwhile, the growing trust she has been feeling for Josh, as they build their relationship carefully after the disaster of Angel's first marriage, is threatened. When Angel finds Josh left for dead in an olive grove at midnight, it seems that this might be the end for them both...

Thrills, hairsbreadth escape after escape, danger, and a full helping of romance, all in the beautiful setting of Corfu, the Paradise island.

"in my opinion this is the best in this series so far."

Tom Elder, USA

"it even excelled its promotion hype. One off the best I have read"

Thea1710, USA

"a fast paced, brilliantly plotted and complex reading experience …

the plot twists and turns will have you on the edge of your seat"

Soooz Burke, Australia

Hel's Heroes

Hel wants a hero like the ones she writes about, but does one exist?

A contemporary romance and an

historic romance in one book!

Helen McFadden – Hel for short – is a success-ful writer of Historic Romance for the eBook market. But one day she decides that she needs to get out and experience a bit of real life. She is soon clubbing, partying and generally having a good time – and men are springing up in her life from all directions.

There's Jason, the actor, Paddy the happy-go-lucky businessman, Jordie the footballer, Markie the pop star, even Pete, her old friend.

But do any of them measure up to the heroes she writes about – espe-cially Jack, the highwayman in her current book?

Will Hel ever learn to relate to a real man and stop expecting to meet a clone of one of her heroes?

"A fast paced, gripping tale of two romances ... and a woman's introduction to real life."

Thea, Amazon.co.uk

"What I enjoyed best ... is the author's ability to put us at Helen's side."

Barbara Silkstone, Amazon.com

"an entertaining book: a real page-turner that brings a smile to one's face"

Ronald W. Sharp, Amazon.co.uk

"an outstanding and cleverly crafted novel ... The twist at the end is awesome."

Rukia the Reader, Amazon.co.uk

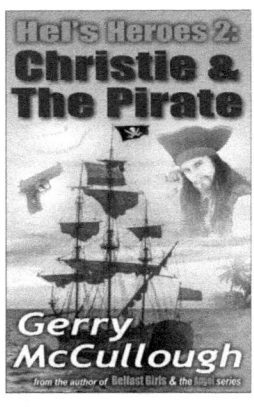

Hel's Heroes 2: Christie & The Pirate

A contemporary romance and an

historic romance in one book!

Christie McCafferty's simple life as a Librarian becomes suddenly complicated when she meets Steve Armstrong. Can she trust Steve or is he a crook?

Meanwhile, Christie is reading a book called *The Pirate* by Helen – Hel for short – McFadden on her *Kindle* at night. In it, Prue is shipwrecked and picked up by a ship flying the Jolly Roger. Prue finds the pirate chief, Black Nick Hawkeye, very attractive. But surely she isn't going to fall in love with a pirate, someone she could never trust?

Christie sees that her own situation, falling for someone who may be a crook, is only too similar to Prue's with 'Hel's Hero', Nick the Pirate. How will it work out for either girl?

A pleasure to read

What a lovely addition to this series. Christie works in the library and her life is pretty smooth and easy. In fact you could say boring, nothing exciting seems to happen.

Then one day she meets Steve and suddenly her life becomes complicated. To make matters even more confusing Christie is reading a book written by Helen (Hel) McFadden about Prue who gets involved with a pirate – Black Nick Hawkeye. While in the real world Christie is trying to figure out if Steve can be trusted, at the same time in the book Christie reads how Prue is also wondering if she can let herself fall in love with Nick.

We are taken on a delightful journey as we follow both Christie and the fictional Prue. Will both find happiness or heartbreak? Have an enjoyable time finding out how it turns out for them.

Ann Stanmore, *Amazon.com*

Not the End of the World

A futuristic, comedy fantasy novel

Gerry McCullough

Sometime in the future, who knows how far away, all the things which people have been dreading and issuing warnings about for years are beginning to happen.

The planet earth has finally become one political unit. Its capital city is now called Nexus Luxuria. Luxury, after all, is clearly the thing most people have been aiming for all their lives.

Life has developed in an almost exactly similar fashion to the threatened forecasts. The world has at last achieved all those marvellous things we've at present only started to acquire for ourselves – global warming; overuse and exhaustion of fossil fuels; a third world with slave labour factories; globalisation of commerce until just seven multi-national companies are running the entire planet (under a titular World President with seven Vice Presidents – a Government with no real power, but considerable wealth and status); and a population kept happy by recreational drugs, which are no longer frowned upon but instead encouraged. In fact, an other-earthly paradise – not!

Oh, and at a guess the future time when all this is happening is about a hundred years ahead of ours.

Or is it only fifty?

"Gerry McCullough combines a fierce and tight narrative drive with humour, imagination and lust. What more do you want?"

Malachi O'Doherty – BBC Writer in Residence, Queen's University, Belfast

"Impressive ... a furious breath-taking pace, followed by a conclusion that has you screaming: Roll on the sequel!"

Sam Millar – best-selling author of ***The Dark Place***, Belfast

Lady Molly & The Snapper

A young adult time travel adventure, set in Ireland and on the high seas
Gerry McCullough

Brother and sister Jik and Nora are bored and angry. Why does their Dad spend so much time since their mother's death – drinking and ignoring them? Why must he come home at all hours and fall downstairs like a fool?

Nora goes to church and lights a candle. The cross-looking sailor saint she particularly likes seems to grow enormous and come to life. Nora is too frightened to stay.

Nora and Jik go down secretly to their father's boat, the *Lady Molly*, at Howth Marina. There they meet The Snapper, the same cross-looking saint in a sailor's cap, who takes them back in time on the yacht, *Lady Molly,* to meet Cuchulain, the legendary Irish warrior, and others.

Jik and Nora plan to use their travels to find some way of stopping their father from drinking – but it's fun, too! Or is it? When they meet the Druid priest who follows them into modern times, teams up with school bully Marty Flanagan, and threatens them, things start getting out of hand.

Meanwhile, Nora is more than interested in Sean, the boy they keep bumping into in the past ...

The Seanachie: *Tales of Old Seamus*

Seven collections of Irish stories, set in the fictional Donegal village of Ardnakil and featuring that lovable rogue, *'Old Seamus'* – the *Séanachie*.

One hundred of these stories have now been published in the popular Irish weekly magazine, *Ireland's Own*, based in Wexford, Ireland.

"heart warming tales ... beautifully told with subtle Irish humour"
Babs Morton (author)

"an irresistible old rogue, but he's the kind people love to sit and listen to for hours on end whenever the opportunity presents itself"
G. Polley (author and blogger, Sapporo, Japan)

*"This magnificent storyteller has done it again.
Each individual story has it's own Gaelic charm"*
Teresa Geering (author, UK)

"evocative characterisation brings these stories to life in a delightful, absorbing way"
Elinor Carlisle (author, UK)

"Like the first collection ... very well written and an effortless read"
Bookworm

"so well written that you find yourself flying through the stories"
Tom Elder (Amazon, UK)

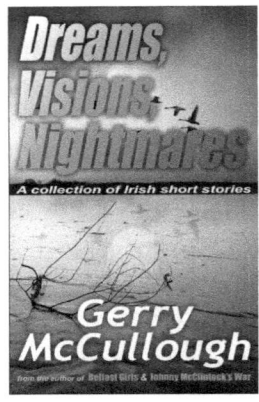

Dreams, Visions, Nightmares

Gerry McCullough

A collection of eight literary and award-winning Irish short stories (newly expanded and edited)

Primroses (winner of *Cuirt international Literary Award*, Galway 2005, published in *West 47* magazine and *Cuirt Annual,* 2005)

Pink Silk (published in *Verbal* magazine, Derry, 2008)

Shadows (published in *Brazen City*, Belfast 2008)

Giving Up (commended in *Seán O'Faolain Short Story Competition*, Cork 2009; published in *Sharp Sticks, Driven Nails*, Dublin, 2010)

Slipping (published in *Ulla's Nib* magazine, Belfast, 2009, winning Star Prize)

Ballystravey, 1988 (published by *Luciole Press*, California 2009; short-listed for *Cuirt Award*, Galway 2010; published in *Crime after Crime* anthology, USA)

Stevie's Luck (shortlisted for the *Brian Moore Award*, Belfast, 2008)

Dark Night (extended into full length novel, *Johnny McClintock's War* – published in 2014)

Non-fiction books from

A Wee Taste a' Craic:

All the Irish craic from the popular
Celtic Roots Radio shows, 2-25

Raymond McCullough

*I absolutely loved this! I found it to be very informative
about Irish life culture, language and traditions.*
Elinor Carlisle (author, Reading, UK)

*a unique insight into the Northern Irish people
& their self deprecating sense of humour*

Strawberry

Ireland – now the good news!

The best of *'Bread'* Vols. 1 & 2 –

personal testimonies and church/fellowship pro-
files from around Ireland

Edited by: *Raymond & Gerry McCullough*

"... fresh Bread – deals with the real issues facing the church in Ireland today"
Ken Newell, minster of Fitzroy Presbyterian Church, Belfast

In Six Hours

... the world changed

Raymond McCullough

In just six hours the Middle East – and the world – will change forever

A friendship forged in war leads four men on separate journeys to their final destiny in a Middle East heading for meltdown

As bitter enemies race towards nuclear conflict, only a miracle can save Israel from the hostile Islamic forces surrounding her. The USA, Russia and the western world are playing with fire in the Middle East, as Iran rushes towards a nuclear climax.

While fighting the Taliban with the ISAF forces in 2012, four young men from very different backgrounds meet in Kabul, Afghanistan:

Shaul *'Solly'* Levine, an Orthodox Jew from New York City;

Micky *'Dev'* Devlin, an Irish Catholic from Boston;

Brandon *'Doubtin'* Thomas, a black Pentecostal from N. Carolina;

Khan Ali *'Zai'* Yusufzai, a Muslim Pashtun from Afghanistan.

They discover that they have more in common than they first thought and make a pact that one day they'll meet up again in Jerusalem after the prophesied Six Hour War in the Middle East, taking separate ways to a common destiny.

Meanwhile, they will keep in touch with one another as much as possible and work towards making that meeting a possibility. Will these prophecies come to pass? Will Israel itself survive the coming nuclear holocaust?

This apocalyptic thriller moves from war, to a couple of budding romances in very different locations, to more war and then the ultimate Middle East war. But even in the midst of conflict, new relationships are being formed. Action, friendship, romance ... and yet more action.

"McCullough writes with conviction and clearly knows his subject well ... [his] fluid prose draws you in and his logic and characterisation make for a believable compelling drama. Highly recommended!!!"
Juliet B Madison, author, UK

"So well written and very descriptive, you actually think you're there. Raymond has obvious knowledge of the areas he has written about as that and his passionate way of writing shine throughout. Must read book"
Tom Elder, author, USA

In One Hour

... Babylon will fall

Raymond McCullough

The debt will be called in and in one hour her destruction will come!

After a devastating, but short-lived, nuclear war, the face of the Middle East – and the whole world – has changed forever! The Ingathering – the world's greatest population transfer – has begun. Huge people groups from India and Myanmar, Pakistan and Afghanistan, from Nigeria, Zimbabwe and South Africa, and many other parts of the world, are all travelling towards one destination.

Four young men, who met first in Kabul, Afghanistan, are re-united in the heat of the logistics of this mammoth operation:

> **Shaul *'Solly'* Levine, an Orthodox Jew from New York City;**
>
> **Micky *'Dev'* Devlin, an Irish Catholic from Boston;**
>
> **Brandon *'Doubtin'* Thomas, a black Pentecostal from N. Carolina;**
>
> **Khan Ali *'Zai'* Yusufzai, a Muslim Pashtun from Afghanistan**.

But meanwhile, not every nation is happy with the Middle East transformation. Back home in the USA, life for Brandon, Dev and their families becomes more and more difficult – and especially so for Shaul's brother, Reuben, and his family.

The world is about to change again – powerful nations are plotting another nuclear holocaust, with one man in charge. Will Shaul and his friends be able to bring out their families to safety – before Babylon falls?

> *"reaching out into new majestic seas ...*
> *it takes a brave writer to take such a step. Keep going. I love it."*
> **Sheila Mary Taylor**, *author, UK & South Africa*

The Whore and her Mother:

9/11, Babylon and the Return of the King

Raymond McCullough

Could the writings of the ancient Hebrew prophets be relevant to events taking place in the world today?

These Hebrew prophets – Isaiah, Jeremiah, Habbakuk and the apostle John, in *The Revelation* – wrote extensively about a latter day city and empire which would dominate, exploit and corrupt all the nations of the world. They referred to it as Babylon the Great, or Mega-Babylon, and they foretold that its fall – 'in one day' – would devastate the economies of the whole world. Have these prophecies been fulfilled already?

Is Mega-Babylon the Roman Catholic Church?
A world super-church?
Rebuilt ancient Babylon?
Brussels, Jerusalem, or somewhere entirely different?
Should this city/nation have a large Jewish population?
Why all the talk about merchants, cargoes, commodities, trade?

Can we rely on the words of these ancient prophets?
If so, what else did they foretell that is still to be fulfilled?
Do they refer to other major nations – USA, Russia, China, Europe?
What about militant Islam?

"AMAZED when I read this book ... in awe of your extensive knowledge on so many levels: Christian, Jewish, and Muslim culture; the Jewish diaspora ... Greek & Hebrew; ... thought-provoking and troublesome ... many will be offended, but you consistently build your case instead of being sensationalistic."
James Revoir, author of *Priceless Stones*

Oh What Rapture!

Is a *'Secret Rapture'* going to spare believers from the tribulation to come?

Raymond McCullough

Arrows bible prophecy series – Book 1

Many are convinced that very soon an event referred to as *'The Rapture'* will take place, where bible believers all over the world will suddenly disappear, leaving society at a loss to explain this disappearance of so many. Many non-fiction books, fiction thrillers and movies have capitalised on this theme, earning a fat revenue for their authors/producers.

But is this really what the bible teaches?
Is *'The Rapture'* genuine, or a deceptive false hope?
Are those who trust in it being duped, so that they fail to prepare themselves for what is coming?
And are they being disobedient to the clear command of the Lord?

Written by the author of *Amazon* best-selling book, *The Whore and her Mother*, also on the topic of bible prophecy, this volume focusses on the false teaching of a *'secret and separate Rapture'* – an event which is NOT supported by scripture!

This book investigates the scriptures used to back up the *'secret Rapture'* theory and clearly compares them to the other scriptures concerning the return of the Messiah, Jesus (Yeshua). The evident truth is revealed and the origins of the false *'secret Rapture'* doctrine are exposed.

Believers around the world are taught to expect persecution, some-times even death, for their faith. More have been killed in the past century than in previous centuries combined – in China, Cambodia, Vietnam, Nigeria, Syria, Iran, Iraq, Egypt, Indonesia, etc. Yet many believers in the west confidently expect to avoid any persecution and be *'beamed up'* out of any coming tribulation!

If you thought believers were soon going to be lifted out of a worsening world situation, be prepared to meet the exciting challenge of scripture head on!

"Interesting and gave food for thought ... definitely worth a read"
Kindle customer, UK

Neighbours from Hell:

Israel and the coming nuclear
attempt to destroy her
Raymond McCullough

Arrows bible prophecy series – Book 2

Facing the Beast:

The man they call the antichrist,
and our response to him
Raymond McCullough

Arrows bible prophecy series – Book 3

www.ingramcontent.com/pod-product-compliance
Lightning Source LLC
Chambersburg PA
CBHW060942120626
46557CB00003B/1104